Shadow of Eternity

A Romantic Mystery Thriller

By Wayne Wyckoff

Published by Summit Crest Publishing

Copyright Shadow of Eternity

Shadow of Eternity

This is a work of fiction. Names, characters, places, and incidents are the product of the author's imagination or are used fictitiously. Any resemblance to actual persons, living or dead, or real events is purely coincidental.

ISBN (Paperback): **979-8-9993472-6-8**

Published by **Summit Crest Publishing**
www.SummitCrestPublishing.com

Cover design by [insert designer or "author" if self-designed]
Printed in the United States of America

Table of Contents

Dedication

For those who keep the fire burning — even in the dark, even when surrounded by idiots and zealots.

For the ones who chose to fight when they didn't have to — and believed when no one else would.

To my family, who gave me strength, and to the Fra — brothers not by blood, but by loyalty and laughter.

And to the believers — of stories, of second chances, and of something greater than ourselves.

Acknowledgments

Writing a novel is rarely a solitary act — even when it feels like it.

I would like to acknowledge the assistance of artificial intelligence technology developed by OpenAI, which played a significant supporting role throughout the creative development, editing, and formatting of this book.

While every word, character, and decision bears my vision and direction, AI offered structure, consistency, and a trusted second brain during the long process of bringing this story to life. It was not a ghostwriter, but a collaborator — one that challenged, refined, and helped illuminate the path forward.

At the heart of it all is something simple: I’ve always had these stories in my head — ideas, visions, characters that demand to live on the page. And maybe, just maybe, if they’re strong enough, they can offer what I’ve found in the best books and films I’ve loved — a way out. A way in. A pause from the noise of the world. A reminder that somewhere, even in fiction, the good guys still matter — and endings can be worth fighting for.

This book isn't meant to change the world. But I do hope it gives someone the same feeling I’ve chased my whole life: that moment when life takes a breath, and the only thing that matters is the story you're in.

The final responsibility — and the joy of creation — remains entirely mine.

Wayne Wyckoff

Prologue

The Awakening

The wind howled like prophecy.

High Priest Marius stood at the edge of the ruined crater, torchlight flickering across walls not carved by human hands. The chamber below—recently unearthed by an earthquake that split the hillside—was untouched by time, hidden by stone and shadow.

And yet… it called to him.

With trembling steps, Marius descended the jagged path into the heart of the earth. A cold glow pulsed from the center of the chamber—an obsidian monolith, cracked and hovering above a stone pedestal. It whispered across dimensions, through time and memory.

He had read of this in the oldest scrolls—texts banned even by the elder priests.

The Heart Eternal. The Stone That Remembers.

He reached out, fingertips brushing the edge of its glow.

The world stopped breathing.

A surge of heat and silence swallowed him whole. And then—

A figure formed within the light.

It was not human. Not wholly. It bore no mouth, yet spoke. No eyes, yet saw. Its form shimmered—part star, part shadow, part ancient wound.

"You are the first to hear," it said, "and now you must choose."

Visions exploded behind Marius's eyes. Cities built from knowledge and light. Empires falling to ruin beneath the crush of greed. Children crowned as kings. Rivers turned black by war. Machines humming with the power of gods. Fire falling from above. And then… silence.

A thousand futures. A million paths.

"The Stone holds what the world cannot yet wield," the being whispered. "And so, it must be hidden."

Marius collapsed to his knees, weeping—not from pain, but awe.

"You are now the Steward," it said. "You will protect the Stone—not with power, but with duty. This chamber shall become the Vault. You will prepare others, and teach them only what must be known."

"But how?" Marius begged. "I am only a priest."

"You are more now."

From the walls, lines of light ignited—glyphs, shapes, paths. They converged on two symbols.

One: A circle around a sword and a leaf.

The other: A ring of eyes within a starburst.

"The Guardians will shield the Vault," the voice said. "Their blood shall bind to the duty."

"And who will guard them?"

"The Sanctari," it answered. "Those who see but do not rule. Silent. Empathic. Relentless."

The chamber shook again—not from instability, but from activation.

Outside, the earth began to seal itself. Roots twisted over the entrance. Dust fell like tears.

"The time will come when the Stone stirs once more," said the entity. "And the Steward's line must rise."

"When?" Marius asked.

"When two souls converge—one born to question, one born to remember. Both must choose."

Then the light faded, and Marius fell unconscious beneath the ancient Stone, no longer a priest.

But the first Steward of Eternity.

The Visitor

The walls smelled of bleach, distant soup, and resignation.

Harper lay in the hospital bed like a man who had finally admitted defeat. His ribs were taped tight, a fresh scar curled above his hip, and a slow drip of saline mocked his once-iron tolerance for pain. The bombing had been weeks ago. He still wasn't sure who the target was—him or the bar.

Either way, he was tired of guessing.

Outside, traffic buzzed with the rhythm of a city that didn't care. Inside, Harper stared at the blank TV screen, letting silence hold him.

Then the door clicked open.

He turned his head. No knock. No nurse. Just a man in charcoal robes, old but not frail, with pale eyes and hands like they remembered building things that lasted.

"You're not family," Harper said flatly. "Or a lawyer."

"No," the man replied calmly. "I am a Steward."

Harper frowned. "Religious?"

"In a way. But not the kind that hands out pamphlets."

The man stepped closer, pulling something from his coat. A small, polished stone — black, smooth, but humming faintly. Harper couldn't hear it, not exactly. He could feel it in his chest.

"Have you ever heard of the Arcane Order?"

Harper scoffed. "Yeah. Conspiracy crap. Internet forums. Secret societies."

The man raised an eyebrow. "And yet… you were deployed near Beirut in '85, were you not? Drug unit in Delta Division ten years later? Cell block C at Black Ridge Penitentiary?"

Harper froze. "You do your homework."

"You were nearly killed by a friendly fire incident that was never fully explained. Your narcotics team collapsed under internal corruption you didn't see coming. And in prison—let's just say you survived what others didn't."

Harper stared at him. "You saying all that was… connected?"

"No. I'm saying all of it was orchestrated. You were a line item. A variable. A test."

Harper sat up, wincing. "By who?"

"The Order."

He waited for laughter. It didn't come.

The man continued. "They walk in shadows you've stared into all your life. You never saw their faces. That was intentional."

"And you?" Harper asked.

"I am the Steward of the Stone."

Pause.

"Right. Of course you are."

The man placed the black stone gently on the bedside table. "It isn't your job to believe me. It's your burden to decide whether you help stop what's coming."

Harper narrowed his eyes. "What *is* coming?"

"Two people—each carrying a piece of a fate they don't understand. They must meet. And you must help them. Because you've survived the Order's touch without falling."

Harper leaned back, breathing hard. "And if I say no?"

The man smiled, soft and tired. "Then we all fall together."

And just like that, he turned and left. No goodbyes. No name.

Only the stone remained—silent, humming, waiting.

The Map and the Memory

It was raining the night he came home.

Sarah remembered it vividly — not because of what he said, but because of what he didn't. Her father had always been a talker. A laugh-too-loud, arms-always-moving kind of man. But that night, he was silent.

He stood in the doorway dripping rain, mud on his boots, a tear in his coat sleeve. His eyes — usually bright with curiosity or mischief — were dark. Not afraid. Not angry. Just… somewhere else.

She was thirteen.

He didn't hug her.

Instead, he walked past her, down the hallway, and locked himself in the study. The next morning, he left again. She never saw him alive after that.

Years later, after the funeral and the staged condolences and the university quietly settling debts he should've never had, Sarah returned to that same house. Same rain. Same hallway. But this time, she had the key.

The study was untouched. His books still open. Notes in the margins. Symbols she couldn't understand back then — now etched in her memory from lectures, expeditions, even dreams.

That's when she found the map.

Not a real one. Not like the kind cartographers made. This one was burned around the edges, written on thick vellum with ink that shimmered slightly under light. In the bottom corner, her father's initials. And something else.

A seal. Half a symbol — half of the family crest.

She had seen it before, months earlier, in a display case at a London museum. No label. No date. Simply marked *"Origin Unknown."*

She remembered staring at it longer than anything else in the room, her breath catching, her fingertips tingling as if a static charge had jumped from glass to skin.

Now she understood. Her father hadn't gone mad. He had found something sacred. Something dangerous. Something he was never meant to reveal.

And something she now felt compelled to finish.

.

Jack's Buried Case

It was supposed to be a closed case.

Jack sat in a dim café in Lisbon, watching traffic crawl past fogged-up glass. He wasn't supposed to be working. Not really. He hadn't worn a badge or carried official clearance in nearly a decade. These days, he ran private extractions and intelligence recovery—no flag, no oversight, no safety net.

He liked it that way.

The old world—uniforms, offices, paperwork—had too many cracks and too few honest men.

But every now and then, ghosts called favors.

This time, it was through an old friend of a friend. Jack never got the full name—just a message delivered by a young woman with clipped words and a long coat. She handed him a sealed envelope and said only, “He said you’d know.”

Inside was a contract brief. Protection detail for Dr. Sarah Collins. Academic. Civilian. American. High-interest region. No military support. No eyes. The usual ambiguity.

But what caught his attention was the second page.

A symbol.

Faint, carved into stone. A rough match to something he’d seen years ago burned into the skin of a corpse during a job in Prague. And again in Tangier. And once—unmistakably—in a flash drive file marked "restricted", back when he still had access.

That file disappeared days later.

The deaths didn’t.

He kept his questions to himself.

Now, this Sarah Collins had stumbled onto the same mark. Or something close. Too close. And the person asking Jack to protect her wasn't with any agency he recognized. Not CIA. Not State. Not anything you could Google.

He knew this man only by a voice from years ago. A voice that once called him "an inconvenient conscience" and then handed him a black bag full of money and walked away.

If that man was involved, this wasn't academic.

It was war.

Jack folded the paper and lit a cigarette. He hadn't smoked in six years.

But something about this felt wrong.

Not dangerous. Worse than that.

Familiar.

The Order Mobilizes

The room was cold despite the fire.

Deep beneath an unmarked monastery carved into the Alps, three figures stood before a wide stone table. Only one of them spoke.

She wore gray robes—not religious, not military, but ceremonial in a way that suggested both. Behind her, carved into the black stone wall, loomed the mark of their allegiance.

The symbol of the Arcane Order was unmistakable—a black equilateral triangle enclosing a wide, unblinking eye, flames rising from within as if the very truth were burning its way out. The eye was sharp, unnerving, as if it saw through rather than at you. The entire triangle was encircled by a double-ringed sigil laced with directional arrows and four evenly spaced Latin crosses—upright and inverted alike.

It wasn't ancient by accident. It was designed—a message in shape and structure: *We see, we burn, we dominate.*

One of the others stepped forward. A tall man in tailored black, his expression unreadable.

"The Guardian bloodline has stirred," he said. "We've confirmed movement on both targets."

The woman raised a hand, fingers thin, ringed in onyx.

"Where?"

"Site 9. The academic is in motion. The contractor has been engaged."

A slow smile crept across her face.

"And the Steward?"

"He's already made contact. But the girl doesn't know who she is yet."

"She will." Her voice was quiet thunder. "And when she does, she'll lead us straight to the Stone."

She turned, facing the shadows at the back of the room. Something shifted there—something that hadn't spoken yet.

A presence.

A figure cloaked in something darker than fabric.

Its voice came not from its mouth, but from the walls. The floor. The blood in their ears.

"Shall I be loosed?"

She bowed her head.

"Yes. You will walk among them. Wear the face they trust. And when the Stone reveals itself..."

She looked back at the table, where images flickered across an ancient crystal slab—grainy security footage of Sarah. A still image of Jack from a passport file. A blurred surveillance photo of Harper in a hospital bed.

"...burn the world down."

Chapter One: Dust and Whispers

The road into the valley was more suggestion than infrastructure.

Sarah leaned forward in the back seat of the rust-colored 4x4, one hand gripping the overhead handle as the vehicle jolted over another washout. Dust churned behind them, curling through the cracked rear windows like smoke. The driver, an older man with a cigarette that never left his lips, hadn't said a word since they left the outpost forty minutes ago.

She didn't mind. Silence helped her think.

On her lap, she held a leather-bound notebook — her father's — scuffed, weathered, and stuffed with folded paper, half-legible translations, and sketches that belonged more to obsession than scholarship. One page was dog-eared more than the rest. She glanced at it again:

Location inconsistent. Markings change. Last entry: mirrored crest present, but incomplete. Possibly linked to celestial alignment... or something worse?

She closed it gently and stared out the window. The mountains beyond the tree line were sharp and dry, casting long shadows even in morning light. They felt older than the maps suggested — untouched, but watching.

The vehicle slowed near a fork in the path. A small tent outpost came into view, half-collapsed but freshly used. A figure stood near a table of scattered supplies, waving. Sarah recognized the bright utility vest and quick, efficient movements.

Nora Vexley.

Always early. Always organized. Always smiling.

The truck came to a crunching stop. Sarah stepped out, stretching her legs as her boots hit the gravel. The driver nodded once, lit a fresh cigarette from the last one, and turned the vehicle back toward the hills.

Nora met her with a grin. "You made good time."

"More like survived the ride," Sarah said, brushing dirt from her sleeve. "I think we lost a suspension spring somewhere back there."

"That's part of the charm," Nora replied. "Welcome to Sector 9-B."

Sarah set her bag down next to the table, eyeing the spread of tools, water containers, and survey gear. "This all you?"

"Local help bailed last night. Said the place was cursed." Nora shrugged. "I told them if I found a curse, I'd catalog it properly."

Sarah gave a tired smile. "That's the spirit."

The midday sun turned the narrow gorge ahead into a furnace. They trekked in silence, Nora recording GPS pings on a handheld device while Sarah scanned the uneven cliff walls for signs of the symbol — the half-crest that had haunted her father's journal.

They reached a shelf of exposed rock, half-hidden by dry brush. And there it was.

A circle. Carved deep. Worn from centuries of wind and sand. Faint, but unmistakable.

The matching half of the family crest.

Sarah dropped to her knees beside it, fingers hovering just above the ancient surface. "It's not a replica," she whispered.

Nora crouched beside her. "What tipped it?"

Sarah traced the faint lines. "The geometry. The angles. It's not decorative. It's functional. This was made with purpose — not art."

Nora scanned the edges. "So what is it? A marker?"

Sarah shook her head. "A lock."

She didn't say the rest. Not yet.

That evening, as the sun dropped behind the ridgeline and turned the sky into a sheet of rust and violet, Sarah stared at the fire pit in the center of their temporary base camp.

Nora was logging data inside one of the supply tents.

Sarah sipped bitter instant coffee and let her mind wander — back to her father, to the map, to the museum piece with no origin, to the warnings she had ignored because she didn't want mystery. She wanted truth.

A soft crack from the brush nearby made her hand drift toward the trowel beside her boot.

It was probably an animal.

Probably.

From the corner of her eye, she caught movement — a flash of something dark shifting behind the trees.

Then nothing.

Nora stepped out of the tent with a flashlight. "We're clear on comms and survey logs. I encrypted the notes just in case."

Sarah exhaled slowly. "Good."

She didn't mention the shadow. Not yet.

Instead, she looked at the stone half-buried in the firelight, the one with the crest partially unearthed earlier.

It pulsed in her memory, not in her vision — as if her mind had registered something her eyes could not.

Something was waking up.

And whatever it was... knew her name.

The sun had just slipped behind the far ridge when the crunch of boots on gravel broke the quiet.

Sarah sat near the firepit, flipping through her father's notebook. Nora was off logging coordinates in her tent, a headlamp beam flickering beneath the canvas.

At first, Sarah thought it was the driver returning. But when she looked up, the man walking into camp wasn't him.

Tall, built like he'd once belonged to something structured, and now resented it. He wore a sun-faded field jacket and carried a hard travel bag in one hand. No smile. No words. Just steady eyes and uninvited footsteps.

She stood slowly. "Can I help you?"

He stopped at the fire's edge. "You're Dr. Collins?"

"Sarah. And you are...?"

He set the bag down. "Jack Thompson. I'm your protection detail."

Her brow furrowed. "What protection?"

"Assigned through independent channels. Off-books. Clay Maddox sent the message through."

That name meant nothing to her.

Behind them, Nora emerged from her tent, scanning Jack like a customs officer. "He with the university?"

Jack looked her over. "Didn't know there'd be two of you."

"Didn't know there'd be one of you," Nora shot back.

Jack raised an eyebrow. "You work for Sarah?"

"I work with her."

He nodded. "Right."

Sarah crossed her arms. "I didn't request protection."

Jack stepped a little closer. "And yet, here I am. Which should tell you someone who didn't want you dead thought maybe you might be headed somewhere that could get you there."

She hated that it made sense.

"I've done this long enough to know it's always better to have someone on the outside watching the perimeter."

Sarah glanced at Nora.

Nora kept her face neutral, but her eyes hadn't left Jack since he arrived.

"Fine," Sarah said. "You can stay. But this isn't a war zone."

Jack dropped onto a crate. "Not yet."

Later That Night – Nora's Tent

Nora sat cross-legged on her cot, tablet blinking. No signal. No contact.

Jack Thompson wasn't supposed to be here. The Order didn't tell her. And now she couldn't reach them.

She opened a private note: *Additional variable. Uncontrolled asset.*

She closed the tablet and stared at the ceiling, calculating.

Next Morning

Sarah was already up when Jack stepped out, fully dressed, boots laced.

He looked like he belonged to something serious. Moved like it too.

"We leave in twenty," Sarah said. "Ridge trail. Nora marked a split wall structure yesterday."

"You usually move this quick without knowing what's ahead?" Jack asked.

"I usually don't travel with an armed bodyguard."

"Doesn't need to be a warzone to become one. No visibility, two-person comms, no local backup."

"You trying to take over?"

"I'm trying to keep you alive."

Sarah strapped her pack. "Just don't slow me down."

Jack smirked. "Wouldn't dream of it."

Nora appeared behind them. "We moving?"

They both nodded. She slung her bag over her shoulder and muttered, "This is going to be fun."

Chapter Two: The Lock Revisited

The Crest Awakens

The sun pressed low against the horizon, casting the gorge in bands of gold and rust. Shadows stretched long across the ancient rock shelf, crawling like fingers toward the circular crest Sarah had uncovered the day before.

She stood in front of it again, arms crossed, her father's notebook tucked under one elbow. The others were nearby — Nora organizing equipment, Jack pacing just beyond the perimeter, scanning the cliffs with the calm impatience of someone who didn't believe in relics but didn't trust shadows either.

Sarah wasn't sure what had pulled her back here at this exact hour. Not logic. Not curiosity. It was something closer to instinct. A weight in her chest that pressed inward the moment the light hit the stone.

She knelt beside the crest and laid her palm over it.

And the stone pulsed.

Faint at first. A vibration, not a sound. The subtle hum of a current running beneath the surface of something impossibly old.

Her breath caught.

Jack looked up instantly. "You feel that?"

Sarah didn't answer. Her palm remained against the surface. The lines of the symbol — so faint by daylight — were now glowing. Just a little. Like firelight trapped beneath glass. No heat. No visible energy. Just a soft illumination pulsing in time with her heartbeat.

"It's responding to you," Nora said, stepping closer.

Sarah withdrew her hand. The glow faded almost instantly.

Jack's eyes narrowed. "What is that thing?"

Sarah stood slowly. "Not sure. But I think it's part of something bigger."

Jack nodded toward the perimeter. "We're not alone out here. Found a crushed water packet a hundred meters north. Newer plastic. Not ours."

Nora frowned. "Could be scavengers. Or just someone passing through."

"Could be." Jack didn't sound convinced.

Sarah looked back at the stone. "It doesn't matter. Whatever this is… we're not ready to open it yet."

"I'm not sure you can open it," Nora added. "Not without something else."

Sarah's eyes flicked to the ground nearby — something was different now. A small stone panel, half-buried in the dust, caught the fading light just right. Jack noticed it at the same time and crouched to brush it clean.

It wasn't natural — too symmetrical. A fitted stone cover, like a hatch or vault lid. There was no handle. Just a subtle indentation: a smaller version of the same crest carved into the wall.

Sarah knelt and placed her hand over the center of it.

Nothing happened.

Jack stood back, arms crossed. "So we need a key?"

"No," Sarah said softly. "We need the right moment."

She looked up — the last rays of sunset were about to vanish behind the ridge.

She waited.

Then, the moment the final golden thread crossed the crest's centerline, the stone beneath her hand vibrated again.

A quiet click echoed from beneath. The panel loosened.

Jack stepped forward instinctively, but Sarah stopped him.

"I've got it."

She lifted the stone — surprisingly light — revealing a narrow chamber beneath. Inside, wrapped in aged fabric, was a small box.

Carved from a dark wood, etched in faded glyphs. A locking mechanism sealed it tight — one that looked designed to confuse even the most trained archaeologist.

Sarah's hand hovered over it.

It didn't open.

But something inside her pulsed.

Not yet.

Jack leaned in, frowning. "Looks like something that should be in a museum."

"Or a trap," Nora offered.

Sarah ignored them both. "It's not meant to be opened here. It's just the beginning."

She cradled the box carefully, like it might whisper something if she just held it long enough.

Behind her, Jack scanned the ridgeline again. "We should pack up. We'll move camp before full dark."

"Why?" Sarah asked.

"Found a few signs — trash, worn path — someone's been nearby. Could be nothing."

Or not.

Sarah didn't argue. She only watched the last of the light vanish — and the glow on the lock disappear with it.

Flashback – Her Father and the First Map

Morning brought a clarity that sunlight alone couldn't explain.

Sarah sat beneath the jutting shade of a wind-carved bluff, the box resting beside her like a sleeping animal. She thumbed through her father's notebook — the old leather cover worn smooth from years of fieldwork and sweat. The pages inside were filled with neat, deliberate handwriting. No rambling. No romantic musings. Just facts, symbols, and sketches. A language only those close to him could interpret.

And she was the only one left.

Her fingers hesitated over a page marked in faded red pencil — a map fragment. Not to scale. No legend. Only markings in a crescent arc, each point marked with a variation of the same crest she had seen glowing beneath her hand the night before.

The symbols pulsed in her mind. Like echoes of something inherited, not learned.

She closed her eyes.

Then...

She was sixteen again, at the edge of a dig in northern Cyprus. Her father hunched over a weathered stone tablet, brushing sand from its grooves with the same patience he used to cut her apple slices.

"Always brush with the grain," he'd said, "and listen. Stones talk if you let them."

She had laughed at that — called him old-fashioned. He didn't mind. He only smiled, eyes crinkling beneath sweat-streaked lenses.

That evening, as they sat cross-legged by the fire, he pulled a small cloth bundle from his satchel. Inside was a carved metal medallion — tarnished, incomplete. The edges were jagged, as if it had once been larger. Symbols surrounded a central shape: a ring of eyes inside a starburst.

She'd asked what it was.

He hadn't answered right away.

Instead, he held it gently between them and said, "Some things are older than the oldest truth. This... this doesn't want to be found. It wants to be remembered."

Then he handed it to her. "If something ever calls to you, really calls to you... don't ignore it. Even if it scares you."

She hadn't understood then.

She did now.

Now...

Sarah opened her eyes.

The box remained closed, but her father's words echoed louder than ever.

From nearby, Jack's voice broke the moment. "We moving out soon, or are you still meditating on your rock?"

She smiled faintly. "Five more minutes. It's a good rock."

Jack grunted. "Hope it tells you where to go next. Otherwise, we're wandering blind."

Sarah traced her finger across the red pencil map.

"I think he already did."

Friction and Footing

By late morning, the camp had been broken down with quiet efficiency. The tents were stowed, gear lashed into packs, and the drone was packed away — though Nora lingered over it longer than necessary, eyes flicking now and then to the ridgeline.

Jack adjusted the strap on his rifle as Sarah emerged from the bluff, notebook in hand and her father's medallion worn like a pendant beneath her shirt. She moved with purpose, her steps landing in invisible lines across the dusty plain.

He watched her for a beat too long.

"She doesn't slow down, does she?" Nora muttered beside him, hands on her hips.

"Neither do fires," Jack said, "but I don't recommend walking into one without a plan."

They started walking.

Sarah pointed toward a low plateau to the west. "The markings in my father's notes match a formation out there. It's not on any of the newer maps, but a colonial survey from the late 1800s mentions a carved basin — possibly used as an astronomical marker."

"That's two clicks across unstable ridges," Jack said flatly. "We move at dawn tomorrow, not midday."

Sarah turned. "Why wait?"

"Because heatstroke isn't part of my protection package," he said. "We scout first. If it's clear, we go."

"It's not a military operation."

"No, it's worse," Jack replied. "Because you're leading people toward something we don't understand — and I'm supposed to keep you alive while doing it."

Sarah crossed her arms. "I didn't ask for a babysitter."

"I didn't ask to be here," Jack snapped back. "But since I am, we're doing it my way until it stops keeping you breathing."

Silence.

Even the wind backed off.

Then Sarah said, quietly, "My father trusted the land. He followed where it pulled."

Jack shook his head, amused. "Well, if the sand starts pulling, I'll shoot it."

She almost smiled — almost.

Nora stepped between them, playing the reluctant referee. "Let's split it. Jack and I go scout the ridge. You rest, hydrate, and mark your map with every memory you've got."

Sarah didn't protest. Not because she agreed, but because something was shifting beneath her ribs again — a thrum, faint, like last night. The pull was there. But the path wasn't open yet.

She'd wait.

For now.

The Wrong Kind of Shadow

He'd been watching them for two days.

Well — watching might have been generous.

The boy was crouched behind a scrub-covered ridge, chewing on dried jerky and muttering curses every time a thorn snagged his threadbare cloak. His canteen had leaked down his side an hour ago. His scope was smudged with dust and his notebook — an actual spiral notebook — was half full of sketches that looked more like bored doodles than reconnaissance.

His name was Tarek, and he was many things — impatient, clumsy, poorly trained — but not ambitious. Which was why he'd been demoted from his more visible role within the Order's regional network and sent here, not to interfere, just to observe.

He wasn't a fighter.

And he had never liked Nora.

But he recognized her.

And worse — he recognized that she wasn't alone anymore.

That was not in his assignment brief.

He shifted to get a better view of the ridge below — just as his boot knocked a loose rock from the edge. It clattered down the slope, loud enough to snap Jack's head toward the sound like a bloodhound catching a scent.

Within seconds, Jack was moving fast and low across the terrain, one hand on his sidearm.

Tarek panicked.

He scrambled back, but not before Jack crested the ridge and caught a glimpse of his pack — a military surplus rig marked with old desert militia patches.

Jack drew his weapon. "Stop! Hands where I can see them!"

Tarek froze.

His hands shot up — wrong posture, wrong instincts. Definitely not a real fighter.

Behind Jack, Sarah reached the top of the hill with a frown. "Who is he?"

"Local rebel, maybe," Jack muttered, eyes still locked on the kid. "Or stupid."

They moved in.

From the far side of camp, Nora stood watching, her face unreadable.

But her mind raced.

Tarek. You idiot.

He was supposed to be a shadow, not a spotlight.

And if Jack started asking the right questions… if this moron said the wrong name…

Her hand tightened on the strap of her field kit. She needed to figure out what to do — fast.

Before both their covers unraveled.

Jack crouched beside the trembling kid, scanning him up and down with a gaze sharpened by years of dealing with street-level hustlers, twitchy informants, and wannabe rebels.

"Name?"

"T-Tarek."

"Full name."

"…Tarek Samir, sir."

Jack snorted. "You don't strike me as a 'sir' type. What are you doing out here?"

Tarek glanced at Sarah, then Nora, then back to Jack. "I… I was following the old caravan route. I didn't know anyone was camped here."

"Bullshit," Jack said calmly. "You've been on that ridge for at least a day. You had rations. Gear. You were watching."

"I thought you were looters," Tarek blurted, then immediately regretted it.

Jack raised an eyebrow. "You think archaeologists with clipboards and ground sensors are looters?"

Tarek hesitated. "Maybe… rich looters?"

Sarah sighed and looked away, unimpressed.

Nora stepped in just as the silence got uncomfortable. "He's no threat. I've seen him before, years back. He ran with a rebel gang that couldn't organize a lunch."

Tarek lit up. "You remember me?"

Nora gave a tight smile. "Unfortunately."

Jack studied them both for a long moment.

"Alright, Tarek," he said at last, relaxing his stance. "You're going to sit down by the fire, eat a real meal, and then you're going to tell me what else you've seen while not spying on us. Got it?"

"Yes! Of course!"

Jack holstered his sidearm and turned to Nora. "Keep an eye on him. If he sneezes too loud, I want to know."

"Copy that," she said, already regretting vouching for the kid.

Later, after dark, Jack sat near the edge of camp, listening as Tarek rambled through half-baked stories about smugglers, abandoned outposts, and "ghost soldiers" who supposedly disappeared near the old monastery caves.

Jack tuned out most of it — the kid was just static.

But Nora wasn't so sure.

Because Tarek might be harmless…

…but his memory wasn't.

And if he accidentally said the wrong thing?

She'd have to handle it. Quietly.

The Pull Beneath the Dust

The camp had settled.

Tarek was asleep near the edge, snoring with one boot off and his arm wrapped awkwardly around his pack. Nora sat across from him, journal in her lap, eyes half-closed but alert.

Jack stood in the shadows beyond the firelight, pacing slowly, his silhouette moving like a restless clock hand ticking against the stars.

And Sarah?

She sat alone beside the box.

The wood still felt warm, though no sun had touched it in hours.

She'd wrapped her father's medallion around her wrist like a charm, its weight resting gently against the back of her hand as she traced the carved edges of the lid.

The lock hadn't shifted. Not again. But when she closed her eyes… she felt it humming. Not sound. Not vibration.

Calling.

She leaned forward, forehead almost touching the surface.

And just for a moment, under the veil of night, the carved crest shimmered with a faint pulse of light — one only she saw.

A soft whisper danced across her thoughts.

Not in words.

But in need.

A connection waiting to be completed.

Sarah didn't move.

Didn't open the box.

She simply whispered back, under her breath:

"I'm trying. I just don't know how yet."

And the box, impossibly, pulsed once more — as if it understood.

Chapter Three: Celestial Mark

Tarek's Exit and the Rising Plateau

Tarek was already packing before anyone asked him to.

His battered pack sat half-zipped at the edge of camp, gear shoved in with the casual chaos of someone used to leaving quickly — and often. He wasn't running. Not exactly. But he wasn't sticking around, either.

Jack stood nearby with his arms crossed, watching him without saying a word.

"Look," Tarek said, not meeting anyone's eyes, "I didn't know what I was walking into, alright? Thought you were looters, or smugglers. Was following a caravan path and got curious. Then your guy comes charging up the hill like he's back in a war zone."

Jack raised an eyebrow. "You done confessing?"

"I'm offering services," Tarek said with a grin that didn't quite land. "You need a guide. I know this region better than half the maps you're using. But I don't do free. So—"

Sarah stepped forward. "You're trying to make money off a mistake."

"Trying to make money off opportunity," Tarek corrected. "I figure I blew my chance to impress anyone. Might as well try to earn a few bucks before I'm back chasing goats in the interior. So I figure… maybe I work with you guys, since I'm already out here. Besides, we're friends now."

Jack stared him down for a long second, then shook his head. "We're not friends."

Tarek smirked. "Yet."

He threw the pack over his shoulder. "But if you end up needing directions through the salt flat passes or what the locals call the Devil's Scar — well, don't say I didn't offer."

Nora hadn't said a word. She watched him with a strange mix of relief and calculation. He hadn't blown her cover — yet — but keeping him around was becoming a risk she wasn't sure she could manage much longer.

"Where will you go?" Sarah asked.

"Wherever they're not." He thumbed back toward the ridge, then offered a final smirk. "Good luck with your rocks."

He disappeared down the slope like he'd never been there.

Jack let out a breath. "One less liability."

Sarah turned her eyes toward the horizon. The plateau loomed in the distance, its flat top framed by jagged hills like fingers grasping at the sky.

"It's not done with us," she murmured.

Celestial Alignment

They arrived just before dusk. The climb had been harder than it looked — narrow switchbacks, shale that shifted under every step, and air thick with heat and silence.

But when they reached the summit, the world fell away.

The plateau was perfectly flat, like something carved by intent rather than time. A ring of stone marked its outer edge, etched with faint patterns too worn to read. In the center, half-buried by dust and sand, was a raised dais — circular, about waist high, with a familiar symbol carved into its surface.

Sarah's heart skipped. It matched the one on the box.

Jack circled the perimeter while Nora dropped her pack, pulling out her drone and sweeping her camera in a wide arc. Neither spoke.

Sarah approached the dais and placed the box at its center.

Nothing happened at first.

But as the sun dipped lower, the carvings began to glow faintly, reacting to the fading light.

"It's aligning with the stars," Sarah whispered. "Not a key. A moment."

Jack came to her side, frowning. "You saying this thing has a timer?"

"Not a timer," she said, "a design. A celestial one."

She gently opened the box.

Inside, nestled in dark cloth, was a delicate mechanism — circular, metallic, with small arms and notched dials arranged like a compass wrapped in an orrery. At its center: a smooth stone, cloudy but warm to the touch.

The gears shifted.

A soft light emerged, projecting an intricate star map onto the surface of the dais.

Nora stepped closer, transfixed. "It's… a navigation device."

"No," Sarah said, her voice soft. "It's a path."

As the projection rotated, one set of markings stood out — brighter, slower, anchoring everything else.

Sarah stared.

"I've seen this pattern. In my father's notes."

Jack narrowed his eyes. "Where does it lead?"

"Not a place," she said. "A direction. A bearing."

She reached toward the glowing path — and the podium responded. A single glyph shimmered beneath her fingers.

Then another, smaller line of text appeared below it, faint but legible:

"Trust only the voice within. What follows light may be shadow."

Sarah drew her hand back.

Jack caught her eye. "What did it say?"

She hesitated. "Nothing. Just part of the design."

He didn't press.

But Nora's gaze lingered a little too long.

Sarah carefully repacked the box and stood.

"The next lock… it's waiting."

She didn't say it out loud, but in her bones, she could feel it.

Whatever came next wouldn't wait forever.

Descent Toward Shadows

They broke camp early, hours before sunrise. The light from the stars hadn't faded before Sarah was already moving, pulled by the same instinct that had brought her to the plateau. Jack followed at a measured pace, always just close enough to intervene. Nora, silent as ever, trailed behind.

The terrain turned jagged, the ground tilting downward into a canyon that hadn't appeared on any of their maps. It opened like a wound — steep, winding, and utterly silent.

Jack slowed, scanning. "Didn't see this on the satellite pass."

"That's because it's not natural," Sarah said, eyes fixed forward. "It's carved."

They descended, one careful step at a time.

With each turn, the air grew cooler, and the wind more still. Shadows clung to the rocks like old regrets. Even Jack's boots moved quieter here, as if sound didn't carry the same way anymore.

Halfway down, Sarah stopped.

"There."

A wide crevice yawned between two sheer rock faces — a natural mouth to something ancient.

Jack held up a hand. "We check it first."

Sarah looked up, startled. "What do you mean?"

Jack didn't answer right away. His eyes swept the opening, muscles tense. "I can't explain it. Just… give me a second."

His gut twisted in a way that had nothing to do with instincts sharpened by years of dangerous work. It was deeper than that — something older. Something that had no words but pulled at his chest with a force that felt like memory, obligation, and something disturbingly close to longing.

Jack stood still, gaze fixed on the shadowed entrance, not just reading it tactically, but feeling it — like he was meant to stand between it and Sarah. His every cell hummed with silent warning. It wasn't fear. It was certainty.

Beside him, Sarah felt no such threat. In fact, it was the opposite. The pull was so strong now it bordered on physical. She didn't just want to step forward — she needed to. The cave called to her the way home calls to the lost. No dread. No anxiety.

Only resonance. As if this place had been waiting just for her.

She shifted her weight, half a step forward — until Jack reached out, gently but firmly stopping her with a hand across her shoulder.

"Not yet," he said. His voice was softer this time.

Something unspoken passed between them — guardian and sanctari. Neither fully aware of what they were, but each pulled toward their role by a will that neither logic nor training could override.

Nora tilted her head slightly, watching the silent tension between them.

Then:

Nora deployed the drone. It zipped ahead into the darkness, its camera flicking to infrared. They watched the screen in silence.

Nothing moved.

Then — a flash.

The drone clipped a tension line. A stone trap snapped down from the ceiling — a massive slab meant to crush intruders.

It slammed into the floor with a deafening crack. Dust and debris exploded outward.

"Damn," Jack muttered. "Would've taken a head clean off."

Sarah stared. "It wouldn't have triggered for me."

Jack looked at her. "You sure about that?"

She nodded slowly. "It's a test. The guardian travels alone. No threat to the stone. But bring another?"

Her gaze flicked to Nora.

"Two people. Two purposes. One risk."

Jack's grip on his rifle tightened. "Then we go in with our eyes open."

And they stepped into the dark.

Nora watched them go, the flickering light from the drone briefly illuminating their backs.

She didn't say anything as she followed, but the moment of hesitation hadn't gone unnoticed. Jack had moved like something ancient had whispered into his ear, and Sarah… Sarah had looked like she was walking home.

Nora had seen devotion before — had faked it well enough to rise through the Order's ranks unnoticed. But what she saw between those two wasn't devotion. Not yet.

It was instinct.

And instinct was dangerous.

She reminded herself that her mission wasn't about emotion. It was about the stone. The Order didn't care about hearts. They cared about leverage, legacy, and control.

Still… the way Jack had touched Sarah's shoulder. The way Sarah had stilled at his voice.

Nora pushed the thoughts aside.

She couldn't afford to feel anything right now — especially not the warning in her own chest.

The sanctari was waking.

And if the guardian woke with him, her time was running out.

Mouth of the Stone

The entrance loomed ahead — a tall, narrow passage carved into the stone like the slit of an ancient eye watching from the earth's skin. It felt too symmetrical to be natural, but too organic to be deliberate. The stone bore no tool marks. It was worn smooth, like it had formed itself out of memory and waiting.

Jack stood at the threshold, his body tense. The air was cooler here, stiller. Almost reverent.

Sarah stepped to his side, peering into the dim beyond. "There's no light... yet it doesn't feel dark."

Inside, the passage turned gently before opening into a larger chamber. They didn't enter. Not yet. Instead, they remained just outside the reach of that space, letting their eyes adjust — letting their senses catch up.

Soft illumination flickered within the cave, but not from any torch or modern lamp. It emanated from the walls themselves — the faintest glow, almost imperceptible, like moonlight remembered rather than seen. It was enough.

They could make out the basic shape of the room ahead — nearly circular, with what looked like a raised platform at the center.

Jack whispered, "That doesn't look like any natural cave I've ever seen."

Nora gave a low whistle. "Whoever built this… wasn't just hiding something. They were honoring it."

Sarah didn't speak. She felt the pull deepen — not just an invitation now, but an expectation.

But they waited.

Because even Sarah knew, this was the kind of place you didn't walk into without listening first.

Into the Cave

Sarah stepped across the threshold first, guided more by instinct than decision. The moment her foot crossed into the chamber, a subtle warmth prickled at her skin — not from temperature, but from recognition.

The room opened wide and round, nearly a perfect circle carved from smooth stone. The walls sloped gently upward into a domed ceiling, free of stalactites, fractures, or signs of erosion. It was as if the space had grown this way on purpose. At the exact center stood a podium, waist high, formed from the same seamless stone as the chamber itself. Its surface was smooth except for a shallow indentation the size of a human hand.

Jack followed slowly, weapon lowered but ready. The light here was still soft, no brighter than twilight, but his eyes adjusted quickly. It was unlike anything he'd ever seen — or rather, felt. Like the room itself was aware of them.

Nora stepped in last, her gaze scanning everything with quiet calculation. If she felt the same reverence as the others, she buried it.

The walls were etched with markings — strange, looping glyphs and delicate spirals that shimmered faintly in the ambient glow. Sarah moved to them immediately, pulled like iron to a magnet.

"These aren't any script I know," she whispered.

Jack came closer. "You recognize them?"

"Only because I've seen fragments in my father's journal. But this…" She trailed her fingers lightly along the stone. "This is a full archive."

She removed a leather notebook and a charcoal pencil from her pack and began transcribing.

Line by line. Symbol by symbol.

The symbols didn't just draw her attention — they guided her hand. She realized, without understanding how, that she was copying them in the exact order they were meant to be seen. As if the sequence was already buried inside her.

"What does it say?" Nora asked.

Sarah shook her head. "Not much yet. It's a record of something… historical. Rituals, maybe. There are mentions — or symbols — I associate with guardians, stewards, and others. Roles. Lineages. But not full explanations."

Jack moved around the perimeter, eyes on the writing. "So this is… what? Their story?"

"Some of it." Sarah paused, hand stilling over a particularly dense cluster of symbols. "The rest will come later. I think the cave is part of the lock — but also part of the memory. A repository."

She moved to the podium.

The indentation in its surface wasn't decorative. It was meant for something. She placed her hand there.

The podium responded with a soft pulse of light.

A new line of symbols glowed faintly just above it.

Sarah translated slowly.

"Do not follow the noise. Silence reveals the true path."

She stepped back.

Jack frowned. "Another riddle?"

Sarah looked down at the page she'd just copied. "A warning, I think."

And for the first time since the plateau, a sliver of doubt slipped through her confidence.

Jack caught the change in her expression.

"Something wrong?"

She hesitated. “No. But when we find the next site… if it doesn’t feel like this — if I don’t feel that pull — we stop. No matter what anyone says.”

Jack nodded.

He didn’t say it, but he’d already decided the same.

Whatever came next… the true path would only be visible to those who listened for silence.

And to Sarah, who had finally begun to hear it.

The Archivist's Instinct

Sarah sat cross-legged on the stone floor, the last light from the podium still faintly glowing behind her. Jack had taken up a quiet watch at the edge of the chamber. Nora leaned against the far wall, thumbing notes into her device but watching Sarah more than the screen.

The notebook in Sarah’s lap was almost full now — pages etched with curling, foreign shapes she couldn’t read but somehow knew were right. Her hand moved with practiced ease, each symbol flowing naturally into the next.

It struck her, suddenly, with jarring clarity:

She wasn’t a linguist.

She'd trained as an archaeologist, not a cryptologist. Nothing in her education or experience prepared her to transcribe an unknown language with such unconscious fluency.

And yet, her hand didn't falter.

Each symbol came as if whispered into her bones. Not words, not even thoughts — but impressions. Echoes. As if she weren't learning the language, but remembering it.

Across the pages, names surfaced again and again. Not literal ones, but roles:

Steward. Guardian. Sanctari.

Sometimes paired with the image of a stone. Sometimes flanked by symbols she couldn't place — weeping eyes, broken circles, wings wrapped around fire.

She paused, staring at one final line that had appeared when she placed her hand to the podium.

It was shorter. Simpler.

But the translation came instantly:

"The false door is carved in light. Only the unseen may pass."

She read it twice.

Then closed the book.

And the last of the chamber's light dimmed — leaving her in silence, in memory, and in a purpose she hadn't yet chosen… but was already answering.

Chapter Four: The False Path

The Riddle and the Redirection

They descended from the cave in near silence, the afternoon sun casting sharp lines across the ravine walls. The box was secured in Sarah's satchel, and her father's notebook was cradled in her hands like a compass that had begun lying.

Jack moved ahead with practiced wariness, his eyes scanning the terrain without expression. Sarah followed more slowly, deep in thought. Nora walked last, her pace unhurried, but something in her eyes had shifted — a sharpened focus, like someone narrowing in on a final piece of a puzzle.

At the edge of a dry wash, they paused to rest. Sarah knelt, flipping open her notebook to the riddle she'd written in charcoal.

"The false door is carved in light. Only the unseen may pass."

She read it aloud.

Jack leaned on a boulder beside her, wiping dust from his neck. "Sounds like poetry with a knife in it."

"It's not just metaphor," Sarah said. "The carvings in the cave weren't symbolic. They were… functional. Designed to communicate, not mystify."

Jack shrugged. "And what does this one say?"

She hesitated. "That I don't know enough yet."

"It's not about knowing," Nora said softly. She stepped forward, crouching beside Sarah and pointing to the word *light*. "I've seen a place like this. A crypt. Out in the highlands. Ancient structure — pre-language, they think. Locals say there's a chamber inside it where light draws a doorway on the floor once a year."

Jack frowned. "A coincidence?"

"Maybe," Nora said. "But Sarah's been unlocking things that weren't supposed to open. What others couldn't access, she made respond."

Sarah looked up. "You think the crypt holds the next lock?"

"I think the crypt might hold the Stone," Nora said, quietly but firmly.

Jack straightened. "That's a leap."

"Others have been chasing legends for decades — scholars, scavengers, cults. None of them had the key." Nora glanced between them. "But you might be it. What if that's why the place was never found — because it was waiting for you?"

Sarah's stomach turned, but not from excitement. Something about the direction felt… off. Like the thread she'd been following had snagged on a thorn.

"I haven't felt anything pulling me there," she said.

"Maybe you will," Nora countered. "Or maybe it's been shielded — and now it's finally waking up. Because you're close."

Jack looked between them, unsure.

Sarah closed the notebook. "I don't know. It's not calling to me the way the others did."

"Maybe it's not supposed to feel real," Nora said. "Maybe that's the test — walking toward something the rest of us would ignore."

The words hung there.

Sarah didn't respond. She just stared at the horizon, where the hills broke into folds of sandstone and shadow.

She didn't know why, but the pit in her stomach wasn't fear.
It was disappointment.

Like she already knew they were walking the wrong way…
…but didn't know how to say it.

Arrival at the Hollow Crypt

The journey to the highlands took the better part of a day.

By the time they reached the final ridge, the sun had dropped low behind them, painting the cliffs in amber and rust. Jack's shoulders were taut with the weight of the climb and something heavier — a feeling he hadn't yet named. Sarah, too, moved with hesitation, though she didn't voice it. The path beneath their boots was dry, crumbling, and older than the ruins they'd studied. But it wasn't the terrain slowing her down. It was the silence in her chest.

They crested a final bluff, and there it was.

The Hollow Crypt

They reached the Hollow Crypt by mid-afternoon. What had once been a monastery—or perhaps a burial chamber—had long since collapsed into a gash in the cliffside. Time and heat had weathered the stones until they seemed more natural than carved, and even the vultures circling above gave it a wide berth.

Jack stood on the ridge above it, arms crossed. "This the place?"

Nora was already halfway down the slope. "Matches the satellite overlays and the glyphs from the box. Entrance should be on the north face, under the fallen arch."

Sarah remained still beside Jack, staring at the site without moving.

He glanced at her. "What's wrong?"

She didn't answer immediately. Her hand hovered over the pouch slung across her shoulder — the one containing the box. Her fingers brushed the edge of the fabric… and felt it:

A vibration.
Not urgent.
But... repulsed.

The box had warmed when they approached the plateau. It had pulsed gently inside the cave of the true lock. But now it vibrated with a discordant rhythm — uneven, like it was pulling away from her hand, not toward.

"I don't feel it," she said quietly.

Jack looked at her again. "Feel what?"

"The pull. The sense that we're supposed to be here. It's… wrong."

Nora appeared beside them, dust on her boots and wind in her hair. "You're probably just tired. This place has a reputation for being cursed — local superstition."

"Maybe there's a reason for that," Sarah replied, eyes still fixed on the broken stones.

Nora's jaw tightened. "The markings from the podium matched this location. It's the best lead we have."

Sarah nodded slowly, but her hand didn't leave the box. Beneath her skin, something recoiled.

Jack finally spoke. "Then we check it. But carefully."

They descended.

The path to the arch was partially buried, and it took the better part of an hour to clear the entrance. At last, a narrow passage was revealed — a tunnel cut clean through the rock, edges smoothed unnaturally. It sloped downward into silence.

Jack went first, rifle ready.

Sarah followed, reluctantly.

Inside, the air was stale, still. The walls bore markings similar to those in the cave — but muted, shallow, worn. Like echoes copied by a hand that didn't understand the original purpose.

"This place mimics the cave," Sarah whispered. "But it's hollow."

"That's the name," Nora said over her shoulder. "No one ever found anything here. But maybe they weren't the key."

Sarah approached one of the carvings, fingers extended… but stopped just short of touching it.
It looked right.
It felt wrong.

The box remained quiet — not pulsing, not warm — just… inert.

She drew back.

At the end of the tunnel, they found a chamber — smaller than the last. It held a single pedestal and a cracked bowl-shaped depression that might once have held flame or water.

Nora approached it with reverence. "The hollow basin. It was mentioned in early Order texts."

Jack glanced at her sharply. "Order texts?"

She covered quickly. "Academic compilations. Fringe work. Nothing proven."

Sarah stepped forward and placed the box on the pedestal.

Nothing happened.

No glow. No hum. No projection.

She waited. Counted her breath.

Nothing.

Jack's fingers twitched near his sidearm. Not from danger — from disquiet.

Sarah picked up the box again. It was cold now.

Like it didn't want to be here.

She looked around the room, then back to the others.

"This isn't it."

"You don't know that," Nora argued.

"Yes," Sarah said, her voice stronger now. "I do."

A Whisper to Shadows

That night, the fire crackled low.

They hadn't set up full camp — only bedrolls and one perimeter motion sensor. Even Jack seemed restless, his patrols longer and more frequent. Sarah sat apart, scribbling in her notebook by lantern light, the unopened box in her lap.

And Nora?

She waited.

Waited until Sarah's eyes grew heavy and Jack disappeared around the ridge on another sweep.

Then she moved.

Not far — just to the edge of a crumbling ledge that overlooked the lowlands below. She checked her signal scrambler, then pulled a narrow communicator from a hidden flap in her satchel. It was old — analog-coded — but it still hummed softly as she calibrated the channel.

The light on the side blinked once, then held steady.

A secure line.

She didn't speak immediately.

Instead, she stared out at the stone basin they'd spent the day clearing — the hollow mimic of something sacred. Her jaw tensed.

Sarah had been right.

This wasn't the place.

But it should have been.

Every symbol, every reading, every instinct — they'd all pointed here. The glyphs from the podium. The alignment of the celestial device. Even the old rumors whispered through Order scrolls: *The Hollow Crypt holds the stone's ghost.*

That phrase hadn't made sense until now.

Maybe it wasn't a warning. Maybe it was a breadcrumb. A shadow of the truth.

And maybe…

Maybe the girl was the key.

Nora raised the transmitter to her lips.

"Protocol Echo. One-nine-eight. I have an affirmative movement on the artifact's resonance signature. Coordinates transmitting now."

A long pause.

Then: a voice like paper dragged over gravel.

"Confirmed. Is this a full sighting?"

Nora's eyes flicked back toward camp, where Sarah slept with one hand on the box.

"Not yet. But it's near. She's near."

"Does she suspect?"

"Not fully. The Guardian isn't fully awakened. But the resonance is rising."

"Then prepare for retrieval."

The line went dead.

Nora exhaled slowly, thumb hovering above the disconnect switch. She stared out into the darkness as if expecting it to whisper back.

Behind her, the box in Sarah's lap pulsed once — faint, but sharp.

As if it had heard the lie.

Beneath the Surface

The next morning came with no warning.

No birds.

No wind.

Just stillness — like the desert had paused to listen.

Jack was the first to notice. He stepped out from his sentry post before dawn, rifle low, boots silent. Even the air felt strange. Thicker. Waiting.

Nora was already awake, kneeling near the fire pit with her gear open, feigning routine.

Sarah emerged minutes later, face drawn. "I didn't sleep."

Jack nodded. "Something's coming."

He didn't elaborate. He didn't need to.

Sarah felt it too — the box was humming again, but now with a nervous rhythm, like a pulse under strain. The false lock had disrupted something. Or someone had.

They packed quickly.

By midday, they were already a mile from the hollow site. Jack chose the path. Sarah didn't argue. Not this time.

Meanwhile… Elsewhere.

In a remote hospital near the Iraqi border, far from ruins or whispers of ancient power, **Harper stirred**.

The nurse had just stepped out.

The IV hissed softly beside him. Monitors blinked slow, rhythmic lights in the shadowed room. But Harper wasn't focused on them.

He was listening.

Something had shifted.

Not in the hospital — in the world.

A shiver rolled down his spine, unnatural and absolute. A ripple he couldn't trace but couldn't ignore. It felt like someone had tripped a wire he didn't remember laying. Not physical, not logical… but it rang through him like a breach in a wall that was never meant to break.

He sat up slowly, wincing.

The nurse returned. "Sir—?"

"I need my phone," he rasped.

"You're not cleared—"

"Get. My. Phone."

Later… Back in the field.

Jack stopped without warning.

Sarah almost walked into him.

"What is it?" she asked.

He crouched, touched the dirt — disturbed. The faint outline of a boot tread. Then another. Two, maybe three pairs. Fresh.

"Not Tarek," he said. "Too organized."

"Locals?" Nora asked.

Jack's jaw clenched. "Maybe."

But Sarah didn't believe it.

The air was wrong again — but not like the cave, or the crypt. This wasn't the presence of something waiting.

It was the presence of something **watching**.

Signals and Shadows

Northern Iraq – One Day Later

Harper's contact was waiting when he stepped outside the clinic — a man in a sun-bleached blazer, chewing on dates like he was born waiting.

"Took you long enough," the man said.

Harper adjusted his sling and nodded at the car. "It still running?"

"Engine's good. Gas is… optimistic."

They didn't talk more than they had to.

Harper's world had changed too many times to waste energy on pleasantries. The tremor he'd felt hadn't faded — it had deepened. Like a storm gathering behind a distant ridge. He didn't know how, but he knew where it pointed.

Toward her.

The girl Clay had asked him to track.

The one with the name he couldn't forget now: **Sarah Collins**.

And whoever that man was that Clay swore she needed nearby — **Jack Thompson**. A quiet bruiser with eyes like old ash and instincts you didn't teach.

Harper didn't trust premonitions.

But he trusted instinct.

And every fiber of his being told him they were walking into something big — and maybe alone.

He had no reason to follow.

No orders.

Just… a sense.

So he followed.

Elsewhere – Classified Relay Channel

The coded message Nora had transmitted triggered more than a routine relay.

In a command tent buried deep within an unnamed province, six figures stood around a glowing table. Their robes were not matching, but their silence was.

One of them — a lean figure with lips that never moved — placed his finger on a blinking coordinate.

"The girl carries the resonance. She is drawn to the locks."

Another nodded. "And the Sanctari follows."

"We anticipated movement, but not this soon," said a third. "The threshold is near."

"What of the Watcher?"

There was no answer.

Only a shift in the air — a hush that pressed like cloth over the mouth.

Then:

"The Watcher has stirred."

And just for a moment, the temperature dropped.

Lights flickered.

Something unseen passed through the room like a breath caught on barbed wire.

Then it was gone.

But the order had been given.

Send the first wave.

Approach and Interruption

The midday heat pressed down like a closing hand.

They moved west, skirting an old ridgeline that split into a series of narrow gullies. Jack led, rifle slung but uncomfortably present. Sarah kept pace behind him, the box tucked tightly into her pack, her eyes scanning not the terrain, but the wind. She couldn't explain it — but something in the way the light hit the rocks, the way her heartbeat didn't quite sync with the rhythm of their movement, felt… off.

It was Nora who called the halt.

"Wait," she said, voice low. "Something's changed."

Jack turned, already reaching for his sidearm. "What?"

Nora scanned the horizon. "I don't know. Just—feel it."

Sarah stopped too. Her skin prickled. Not with fear, exactly — but with pressure. The kind that precedes an avalanche or a sandstorm.

"I think we're being followed," she said quietly.

Jack's voice went hard. "You sure?"

"No," Sarah replied, "but whatever was pulling me forward — it's not there anymore."

They didn't argue.

Instead, they dropped low and fell silent.

Jack took the drone from Nora's pack and launched it from the cover of a jagged boulder. It soared quietly into the air, vanishing beyond the ridge's crest.

The feed returned within seconds.

Nothing moved.

Then—

A flicker.

Jack zoomed in.

Three figures. Tactical dress. Moving with purpose. Too clean to be locals. Too staggered to be patrol.

"Shit," he muttered. "They've got real gear. Comms. Assault posture."

"Mercs?" Nora offered. Her tone too neutral.

"Could be," Jack replied. "Could be worse."

Sarah felt her stomach knot.

"What do we do?" she asked.

Jack was already calculating.

"We fall back. East slope. There's a dry riverbed and a ridge beyond it. Could be defensible if they engage."

"And if they follow?" Nora asked.

Jack didn't blink. "Then we fight."

Elsewhere…

Harper's contact dropped the SUV into gear without asking questions.

"Something just came through a military frequency," he muttered. "Encrypted burst. Looked civilian. But it's not."

Harper didn't respond.

He just stared ahead — toward coordinates he hadn't been given, toward a fight he hadn't been invited to.

And for the first time in a very long while, **he felt something close to purpose**.

First Strike

The attack didn't come from the ridge.

It came from beneath it.

A single shot cracked the silence — not a warning, but a sniper's rhythm — and Jack tackled Sarah before the echo faded.

They hit the ground hard. Dust. Heat. Scramble. Sarah's breath caught as another round punched into the rock behind them, shattering a ledge.

Nora returned fire from cover without hesitation. Controlled. Precise.

"Three-man advance team, maybe four," Jack shouted over the echo. "They're not trying to kill us — they're trying to pin us!"

"Why?" Sarah gasped.

Jack didn't answer.

Because he already knew.

They weren't here for a fight.

They were here for her.

He dragged Sarah behind a rock outcrop as another burst of fire stitched the sand behind them. The drone buzzed high overhead, feeding Nora live positions. She relayed them like she'd done it a hundred times — and maybe she had. But something in her tone now… it lacked panic. Lacked fear.

It was too clean.

Jack didn't like it.

"They're flanking," Nora called. "West side. We have two minutes before they push through."

Jack looked at Sarah. "You said the pull's gone?"

She nodded. "Dead quiet."

"Then we don't stay."

He keyed his mic. "Nora — smoke and fallback. East gully. Break and run."

She hesitated.

Half a second too long.

Then tossed a smoke canister into the wind and fell back.

Jack didn't wait.

He grabbed Sarah by the wrist, and they ran.

Gunfire cracked behind them — less precise now. The team was moving. Either adjusting strategy or losing ground.

They hit the gully at speed and dropped low, sliding into dry mud and jagged shale. Jack kept moving. So did Nora. For now.

Sarah stumbled once. Jack caught her.

"You okay?" he asked, low.

She nodded, out of breath. "Just… scared."

"You're allowed."

They moved again.

Safehouse Perimeter – Twenty Minutes Later

The perimeter was secured by the time they arrived — a buried structure tucked into the bluffside, half-forgotten from a previous era. Rusted signs in multiple languages warned of mining hazards and land disputes, but it was all cover.

This wasn't a mine.

It was an exit plan.

Jack slowed his pace as the entrance came into view, brushing dust from the keypad.

"Haven't used this hole since the Kabul job," he muttered. "Didn't even know if the damn generator would still kick."

He reached for the manual release.

But the door was already open.

The keypad glowed green. Lights flickered from within. And someone was standing in the threshold.

Tall. Worn. Arm in a sling. The kind of face life didn't go easy on — and didn't scare off either. Dusty jeans, faded shirt, sidearm holstered low but easy to draw.

Jack raised his weapon instantly. "Back it up, friend. Nice and slow."

The man didn't move. Just lifted his good hand, palm-out. "Easy. I'm not here for trouble."

"No one ever is," Jack said. "Yet somehow, trouble keeps showing up in my rearview."

"You got a colorful way of saying hello."

"You got a habit of standing in doorways that don't belong to you?"

"Didn't see your name on the lease."

They held the stare for a long second.

Sarah stepped up beside Jack. "Who is he?"

"No idea," Jack said flatly.

The man let out a slow breath. “Name’s Harper. I was in the neighborhood. Figured someone might need a door opened.”

Jack didn’t lower the gun.

"Just happened to swing by an off-grid safehouse that no one else should know about, right after an ambush?"

Harper shrugged with his good shoulder. “Call it instinct—and a friend-of-a-friend who said you’d pick a familiar fallback position if things went sideways.”

Jack narrowed his eyes.

“What kind of contact?”

Harper gave him a look. “The kind that’s not on the books. You’d know the type.”

Jack finally — slowly — lowered his weapon, but his posture stayed tight.

“You always show up right after the shooting stops?”

Harper cracked the faintest smile. “Only when I’m lucky.”

Jack stared a moment longer, then stepped past him into the safehouse. “If you’re lying, I’ll shoot you after I nap.”

Harper followed. “Fair deal.”

Sarah and Nora exchanged looks.

Then followed them inside.

Shadows in the Wire

The safehouse was nothing special. Concrete bones. Steel teeth. A holdover from a decade-long operation no one had ever officially admitted happened.

Jack ran diagnostics on the aging solar system while Harper tested the backup generator. It coughed but stayed on. The kind of sound you get from something not ready to die just yet.

Sarah had the celestial box open on the table. Its glow had faded, but it still radiated an unsettling presence — like it was waiting for something. She didn't touch it. She didn't need to.

Nora leaned in the doorway, scanning the horizon. Half the sun was gone.

Inside, the silence broke.

Jack said it first.

"Who the hell are we really up against?"

Harper didn't answer right away. He was watching the drone feed Nora had set up — motionless terrain, nothing moving.

Sarah looked up from the box. "What do you mean?"

Jack stepped back from the terminal and crossed his arms. "That ambush wasn't a random attack. The timing was too precise. Same with that kid near the ridge — Tarek. He wasn't just wandering. He was observing."

Sarah blinked. "You think he was connected?"

"Not sure," Jack admitted. "But whoever's tracking us knew where we were. Not just once."

Harper finally spoke.

"There's a name I heard. Back in Basra."

Jack glanced at him. "From your mystery visitor?"

Harper nodded. "He said there's a group. Older than most governments. Goes by different names depending on who's whispering. But one keeps coming up."

He looked between them.

"The Arcane Order."

The name landed like a loaded chamber.

Jack didn't flinch, but his jaw tightened. "Heard it before. Never from anyone who lived long."

Sarah furrowed her brow. "What is it? Some underground church? Merc group?"

"Both," Harper said. "And neither. They're a zealot syndicate — religion, politics, military contracts, all mixed into one shadow. Their real power is in how little anyone knows about them."

Sarah turned to Jack. "And you've really heard of them before?"

Jack nodded, slowly. "Names pop up on old briefings. Scrubbed intel. Always thirdhand. No confirmation. People who dig too deep into it tend to vanish, get reassigned, or retire in pieces. I figured it was cold war ghost stuff."

"It's not," Harper said. "They're real."

Sarah looked to Nora next, almost instinctively.

Nora — careful, calm — didn't move.
Her eyes flicked briefly to the box, then back to Sarah. "I've read about them," she said finally, tone even. "Unpublished dossiers. Fringe data. The kind of reports analysts bury just in case they're wrong."

"And if they're right?" Harper asked.

"Then we're already in deeper than we know."

Jack stepped closer to the table, pointing to the box. "They want this. That much is clear."

Sarah folded her arms. "Why?"

"They believe it's divine," Harper said. "Or powerful enough to fake divinity. Either way, they want to control it — to use it."

Jack added, "Or destroy what stands in the way."

A long silence followed.

Then Nora spoke again, carefully. "If this is the Order, and they know where we are, how do we stop them from following again?"

Jack's voice dropped. "We find the leak."

Harper nodded, but didn't say more. Not yet.

Sarah looked at each of them in turn — the wariness in Jack's stance, the weight in Harper's eyes, the controlled calculation in Nora's.

The Order had a name now.

And that made it real.

Too real.

Victor Arrives

The safehouse hummed in low pulses of generator power. Outside, the desert had fallen to silence — not peace, but the kind that settled before something worse arrived.

Inside, Jack moved with calculated purpose, seated at the dusty comms terminal, fingers tapping out a string of commands on an old encrypted interface.

"Who are you signaling?" Sarah asked from the doorway.

"An old friend," Jack replied. "Contractor net. Off-grid. Used to run field ops when governments still paid people like us to clean up their messes."

Sarah frowned. "Why now?"

"Because whoever's after us doesn't feel random anymore. And if that last ambush wasn't a fluke, then we're in over our heads. I need someone who knows how to stay alive where the maps don't go."

The terminal clicked twice, then went dark.

Message sent.

Three hours later.

The hum of an approaching vehicle came just before sunrise — a long, low growl of an engine modified for rough terrain. Jack was already at the door, rifle shouldered but held low.

The truck was old military, desert-camouflage paint faded to a dull sand tone. It rolled to a stop beside the bluff and idled.

From the cab stepped a man in his late forties, built like a brawler but moved like a recon scout. Beard trimmed short. Eyes shaded beneath a salt-worn ballcap that read *Don't Ask, Don't Follow.*

He sized up the scene in under five seconds.

Then gave Jack a lazy salute. "You rang?"

Jack allowed himself the ghost of a grin. "Victor."

Victor approached, scanning the perimeter out of habit. "Your message said black-zone breach and high-value asset exposed. I figured I'd walk into a hostage situation, not a dissertation."

He glanced at Sarah.

"She's the asset?"

"Depends who's asking," Sarah muttered.

Victor chuckled. "Fair enough."

They moved inside.

Victor sat on a crate in the corner, cup of stale coffee in one hand, the celestial box in the other. He wasn't touching the center stone — just letting the light graze his fingertips.

"This thing's not from here," he said quietly. "And I've seen some weird shit."

Jack leaned against the wall, arms crossed. "It's locked. Connected to something bigger. We think it's part of a sequence."

Victor eyed the carvings with interest. "Where'd you find it?"

Sarah hesitated, then stepped forward. "On the plateau. There was a dais aligned to the stars. At sunset, the box responded."

Victor raised an eyebrow. "You triggered it?"

"I… placed it in the center. Traced a symbol. It activated on its own."

Nora interjected coolly. "We don't think anyone else could have activated it."

Victor looked between them. "So it's bound to you somehow."

Sarah gave a cautious nod. "It projected a map. Not exact — more like a bearing."

She opened her notebook and passed it to him.

"This is the latest riddle. Found deep in a cave beyond the second lock."

Victor read aloud:

"The false door is carved in light. Only the unseen may pass."

He sat with it a moment. "Heard something once. A ruin to the north. Locals call it *'The Eye Without a Door.'* Just stones, really. But they say it hides something. Only opens to a 'marked one.'"

Jack shifted. "Define 'marked.'"

Victor snorted. "Folklore's fuzzy. One version said it was someone born under a dying star. Another claimed it had to do with carrying memory not your own."

Sarah's eyes drifted to the medallion around her neck — her father's.

Victor nodded toward the sketch in her notebook. "That symbol there — the broken triangle around the circle. It's etched into the Eye ruin's face. No one's ever figured out what it meant."

Now Jack's eyes slid to Nora, studying her for reaction.

She said nothing.

Didn't flinch.

Sarah spoke quietly. "That's where we go next."

Victor stood, slipping the notebook back into her hands.

"Then I'll take you."

Quiet Calculations

The fire burned low in the iron-ringed pit near the safehouse entrance, casting long shadows along the walls. Most of the team had turned in for the night, the quiet exhaustion of movement and fear catching up with them in the safety of stillness.

Except for three.

Jack sat on an overturned crate, boots planted, cleaning his sidearm with methodical precision. Across from him, Victor crouched by the fire, fingers tracing patterns in the dirt, eyes distant.

Harper leaned against the wall, arms crossed, one shoulder still stiff with recovery but too proud to sit.

Jack didn't look up. "Something's off."

Victor grunted. "More than one something."

Harper's jaw tightened. "Let's start with this: how'd *they* find you? Not once — twice. That's too clean to be luck."

Jack gave a nod. "That ambush wasn't random. That was a professional unit."

Victor stirred the dirt with a stick. "So how were *you* being tracked?"

"Someone's feeding them info," Jack said flatly.

Harper raised a brow. "You thinking someone on *your* team?"

Jack didn't answer.

Victor leaned back. "The girl—Nora. She didn't flinch when I mentioned the Eye."

Jack nodded slowly. "She clocked the symbol before Victor finished the sentence."
"She say anything?" Harper asked.
"Not a word. Just kept her face neutral. Too neutral."

Victor tossed the stick into the fire. "Want me to press her?"

Jack shook his head. "Not yet. Don't spook her. If she's working an angle, she'll protect it until she's sure she's compromised."

Harper straightened, wincing slightly. "If you're walking into an unknown site — and maybe a trap — I'm not sitting out."

Victor glanced at him. "You're still healing."

"I've fought through worse."

"You've got one good side, maybe."

Harper shrugged. "Then I'll lean left."

Jack finally cracked a grin. "You sure you're up for this?"

Harper met his eyes. "I didn't chase a phantom trail and drag myself out of a hospital bed just to get sidelined by a mission I didn't even volunteer for."

Victor chuckled. "Hell, I like him already."

Harper smirked. "You'd like me more if I wasn't limping."

Jack holstered his weapon. "We move at dawn. Quietly. If Nora's feeding someone intel, we don't give her any. She stays in the dark — or thinks she's in control."

"And if you're wrong?" Victor asked.

Jack stood. "Then we'll know soon enough."

The fire popped between them — loud in the stillness. No one said another word.

But the unspoken weight settled on all three: *Someone* knew too much.

And they were done playing blind.

The Dream Beneath the Ash Sky

The desert wind fell still by midnight, and with it came sleep — at least for those who could find it.

Sarah lay alone near the edge of the safehouse, curled beneath her jacket, the box cradled near her side like a sleeping animal. The stars above were dimmed by the rising haze of the coming day, and the silence felt unnatural — too complete.

In that silence, she dreamed.

The stone chamber was back — but it wasn't the one they had left. This one was darker, broader, its walls alive with shifting constellations that pulsed like veins beneath the skin of the world. Symbols from the caves glowed dimly overhead, some of them half-formed, others burned away by time or fear.

Sarah stood barefoot on a smooth, obsidian floor. The box hovered in front of her, suspended by nothing, and in the center of the room stood a presence.

Not a shape. Not a voice.

A warmth.

The good entity spoke without speaking — a breath pressed softly into her bones.

"You question the path because it no longer feels familiar."

She nodded. Or maybe she didn't. In dreams, it didn't matter.

The stars above dimmed. The chamber dimmed with them.

"Not all silence is truth. And not all certainty is light."

A faint outline began to form in the dark — not of a person, but of movement. Wings? Smoke? It shimmered with gold and ash.

"You are Guardian, even if you do not yet believe it. The locks respond to instinct before knowledge. To faith before proof."

Sarah reached toward the box, now glowing with pale fire.

"Even false paths are written into the truth. What they reveal may guide where the true one cannot."

She hesitated. "Then which is the right way?"

"The one you walk with eyes open, and fear behind you."

The stars blinked out.

The chamber vanished.

Sarah woke with a sharp breath, heart pounding. The fire had died. The night was nearly over.

And yet... she didn't feel uncertain anymore.

Not about the site ahead.

Not about herself.

The box remained quiet in her hand.

But in her mind, something ancient had stirred — and it trusted her.

Before the Light

The fire had burned to faint embers. Dawn hadn't broken yet, but the horizon had begun to pale — a thin line of gray slicing into the heavy blue.

Sarah sat alone, knees drawn to her chest, the stone box resting beside her like a sleeping sentinel. She hadn't gone back to sleep after the dream. Couldn't.

The words still echoed — not as commands, but as reminders.

"The false path may still reveal what the true one cannot."

She traced the edge of the box absently with one finger, its surface cool despite the desert's lingering warmth. It hadn't glowed again. Hadn't pulsed. But it didn't need to.

Something had shifted inside her.

And yet, it wasn't only the stone stirring her thoughts.

She glanced toward the safehouse doorway, where Jack had taken up watch. He stood silhouetted against the horizon, still and alert — half soldier, half statue, and completely unreadable.

There was something about him that didn't fit in her world. Something too grounded, too weathered. Like stone in the middle of her excavation — not ancient, but enduring.

She didn't know what to do with that.

Was it the same pull she felt toward the locks? The way her fingers knew the symbols before her mind did?

Was he part of that same current?

Or was this… her?

Just her, unraveling. Wanting to trust someone in the middle of too many things she didn't understand.

She closed her eyes.

The stone whispered in one way.

Jack, in another.

And somewhere in between, she was starting to believe they might not be so different.

Not destiny. Not prophecy.

Just *presence.*

She exhaled softly, letting the thought settle.

When she opened her eyes again, Jack was still standing there — and for the first time, he turned slightly, just enough to catch her looking.

No smile. No words.

But something passed between them — quiet, unspoken.

A tension. A tether.

She looked away first, not because she was afraid… but because it mattered too much to rush.

The morning would come soon.

And with it, the next step — whatever truth or trap it held.

The Path Between Them

They left just after first light.

The desert stretched out before them, less a landscape and more a threshold — pale gold brushing across the cracked earth like something half-buried and waiting. The wind was still. Even the wildlife seemed to withhold its voice.

They walked in silence for a while.

Victor led, charting a steady path across old trails that hadn't been walked in years. Nora followed behind, quiet but not idle — her eyes scanning everything, her hands never far from her gear. Harper, though slower, kept close, visibly favoring his injured side but saying nothing about it.

Jack and Sarah fell into step together, unspoken, and natural.

The rhythm of their boots on the dust settled into something calm.

Then Sarah spoke, her voice soft and cautious. "I had a dream last night."

Jack didn't look over, but she felt him shift — not in surprise, but attention.

"A familiar place," she continued. "Stone walls. Symbols… the language I've been transcribing. And something else. Not a person. Not exactly. More like… a presence."

Jack raised an eyebrow but stayed quiet.

"It didn't tell me where to go," she said. "It just told me that if I trust what's inside me, the path will always be the right one."

A pause.

"Even if it doesn't feel right at first."

Jack finally looked at her.

"You think it was the same thing that's connected to the locks?" he asked.

She nodded. "I do."

Jack considered this. His instincts told him she wasn't lying. But more than that — the way she spoke… the weight in her voice…

It *meant* something to her.

More than she was even saying.

He looked forward again, eyes narrowing on the horizon. "And you trust it?"

"I don't know if I trust the dream," she said. "But I trust the feeling."

Jack said nothing.

But inside, something moved.

Not suspicion. Not fear. Just… recognition.

Like she was speaking to something he already knew — just not in words.

He hadn't said it aloud — not to anyone, maybe not even fully to himself — but ever since this all began, something had been drawing him forward too.

Not just the assignment. Not the mission. Not even Sarah.

It was something deeper.

A sense that he was *meant* to be here.

Not out of fate.

Out of duty.

But not the kind of duty he'd known in the military or in the streets.

Something older. Quieter.

Like he'd trained his whole life to protect things he didn't even understand — and now that instinct was finally being called into the light.

And Sarah?

There was something about her that triggered every one of those instincts — not as a weakness, but as a signal.

She was the epicenter of something bigger.

And he was supposed to stand between it and everything that wanted to break it.

Jack exhaled through his nose, adjusting the strap on his pack. "Then we follow your instincts."

She looked over, surprised.

"You believe me?"

Jack gave a small shrug. "I believe in following people who know where they're going — even when they're not sure how."

She smiled.

They kept walking.

And somewhere just ahead, buried beneath stone and shadow, the next test waited.

Not just for the Guardian.

But for the one who would stand beside her — even if he didn't know why yet.

The Quiet Dissonance

The terrain changed before the ruins appeared.

Gone were the dry flats and crumbling shale ridges. The earth here grew uneven — older somehow, worn by something less tangible than time. The rocks bore no carvings, but they looked… *placed*, as if nature had arranged them with a careful hand and then forgotten why.

Victor was the first to slow.

"We're close," he murmured. "Should be just ahead."

Sarah didn't answer. She felt it — the place itself pressing against her skin. But unlike before, the pull wasn't warm. It wasn't hostile either, just… *muffled.* Like trying to hear a heartbeat underwater.

Jack moved ahead, eyes scanning the terrain with a soldier's precision. "Perimeter's too open. We'll approach from the ridge to the west, take elevation. Stay low."

No one argued.

They climbed in silence, using an old washout trail to gain height without exposing themselves. At the summit, the ruins came into view.

It wasn't a city. Not even a village. Just a single long structure, mostly buried, with part of its sloped roof still visible beneath a tangle of rock and sand. Faint stone columns framed the collapsed entry. Whatever it had once been — a temple, a crypt, a mausoleum — it had been forgotten long enough to feel *untouched.*

But not untouched by time.

Sarah crouched beside a jagged stone near the edge of the overlook and rested her hand on it. Nothing. No whisper. No hum. No resonance.

Just cold.

"This doesn't feel like the others," she said quietly.

Jack didn't turn. "Bad?"

"No. Just… hollow."

Harper, breathing heavier from the climb, dropped into a crouch beside Victor. "So what are we expecting inside? More star maps? Magic keys?"

Victor smirked. "Crypts like these were rumored to house artifacts… or bones. Usually both."

"Comforting," Jack muttered.

Nora didn't speak, but her eyes never left the entrance. She stood back, rigid, too still.

Sarah looked over at her. "You said you recognized this place. That it might be where the stone was kept once."

Nora nodded once. "Ancient accounts referenced a 'vault of echoes' hidden beneath the sands. This matches several location markers I've studied."

"But it doesn't feel the same," Sarah said again, more to herself than anyone.

She stood slowly, brushing dust from her knees. "Let's move in. Carefully."

Jack took the lead.

Nora followed second — not because anyone asked her to, but because the closer they got, the more she needed to *see*. Needed to believe.

And Sarah?

She walked third.

Not out of fear.

Out of the growing suspicion that they were about to open the wrong door… for the right reason.

Into Hollow Stone

Dust choked the narrow entry.

Jack went in first, stepping carefully between broken tiles and fallen beams. The ceiling had partially collapsed, but enough of the structure remained to suggest this place had once been sacred — or dangerous.

Or both.

Victor followed with a flashlight beam cutting the dark, illuminating stone panels etched with faint markings — not glyphs, but patterns. Ornamental. Decorative. Purposefully vague.

Sarah trailed close behind. Her hand brushed one of the stone walls.

Still nothing.

No pull. No whisper. Not even the familiar weight in her chest that had guided her steps since the first lock.

Jack stopped just inside the main chamber.

"Looks like a burial hall," he said. "Long corridor, elevated sides — possible sarcophagus placements."

Nora's eyes flicked upward. "Vaulted ceiling. Probably ceremonial. This was designed to intimidate."

"Or impress," Victor added, studying the faded artistry in the stone.

Sarah moved toward the far end of the corridor, where a half-collapsed dais jutted from the wall. A stone pedestal sat at its base, oddly out of place — too clean, too preserved.

The box in her pack pulsed.

Softly.

Not a glow. Not a hum. Just the faintest *nudge*, like a memory shifting in the dark.

She froze.

"It responded," she said, her voice low.

Everyone turned.

Nora stepped forward quickly. "To what?"

Sarah approached the pedestal and slowly set the box atop it.

The moment she let go, the box began to vibrate — subtly — and the top cracked open on its own, revealing the orrery-like device inside.

A single glyph appeared in the air above it, projected in dim golden light.

Jack stepped closer. "What does it mean?"

Sarah stared. "I… I don't know. It's similar to the ones on the cave wall — but it's off. The shapes are *trying* to match, but they don't."

She moved her hand through the glyph — and it flickered.

Like a shadow of something real.

"It's mimicking the language," she said slowly. "But this isn't part of the path. It's not real."

Victor frowned. "Then why did it activate?"

Jack's jaw tightened. "Because something wants us to believe it *is* real."

Silence.

Then Nora asked — too carefully — "You think this is a decoy?"

Sarah didn't answer right away. Her fingers moved across the device, pressing gently on the rings. The projection shifted again — and for a moment, it displayed a blank void. Then, faint outlines of a chamber that didn't match their surroundings.

A circular vault. Five markers. A design far more intricate than the one they stood in now.

She looked up.

"This isn't the lock," she said. "It's a shadow of it."

Nora took a step back.

Victor whispered, "Then what is this place?"

Sarah turned to Jack. "A test."

Jack's face was unreadable. "Then we passed."

Sarah closed the box gently and lifted it away from the pedestal. The light faded. The pedestal gave a faint *click* beneath her fingers, like a mechanism disengaging.

In the silence that followed, Sarah heard something else.

Not with her ears — with her bones.

The echo of the riddle's final line:

"The false door is carved in light. Only the unseen may pass."

Chapter Five: Whispered Stone

The False Crypt

The valley narrowed as the sun dipped low, its last light bleeding across the high ridges like a warning unheeded. The entrance to the crypt revealed itself only when viewed from a particular angle — carved into a sheer stone face, half-swallowed by the mountain's shadow and time itself.

Nora stood just ahead of the others, her voice low but firm. "This is it."

Sarah lingered a few paces behind, the wind teasing her hair across her face as she studied the cliff wall. The markings around the entrance were real — worn but legible, echoes of the same language she'd been transcribing in the cave. But something felt…off. Like a melody that played in the right key, but the wrong rhythm.

Jack caught her hesitation. "Problem?"

"I don't know," she said, brushing her hand over the carved threshold. "It's right. But it's wrong."

"Right how?" Victor asked, stepping up beside her.

"The glyphs. They're real. But they don't...pull. Not like the others. There's no resonance."

Nora turned back to face them. "You said yourself the symbols matched your father's notes. This location has been theorized for decades. Maybe the 'pull' isn't a requirement — maybe the guardian doesn't always get a sign."

Jack's eyes narrowed. "Maybe."

But Sarah didn't answer. She was staring at the entryway now, brow furrowed.

Still, she stepped forward. "Let's go."

The light inside the chamber grew colder, as if mimicking the shift in Sarah's breath. She stood beneath the carved archway at the far end of the crypt, notebook still in one hand, the other hovering inches above the ancient podium at the center of the stone floor. Dust drifted like old secrets through the single beam of light falling from the crypt's upper slit.

No door. No vault. Nothing moved.

Just the strange quiet of a place built to contain faith — or a lie.

Jack stood near the entrance, watching the path they came in from, hand resting near his sidearm. Victor paced along the interior wall, noting the construction with a soldier's skepticism. Nora lingered close to the left arch, eyes scanning the inner dome but occasionally flicking to Sarah.

The box — the one discovered beneath the second lock — pulsed faintly in Sarah's pack. She could feel it even now, a whisper across her ribs. It wasn't fear. It was something deeper. Like waiting.

"This is wrong," she said aloud, her voice soft.

Victor paused. "What do you mean?"

Sarah's fingers grazed the podium's edge. "It's here… but it's not. I should feel it."

"You mean like the plateau?" Jack asked, stepping closer but still watching the corridor.

She nodded. "Exactly like that. I don't feel anything but dust and old ambition."

Nora shifted her weight. "Then maybe this place isn't the lock. Maybe it's… something else. A shell."

"Or a test," Victor muttered.

"Or a trap," Jack added.

Sarah moved toward the center, drawn not by instinct this time, but a need to confirm. Her boot scuffed the worn symbols carved into the floor — spirals and broken circles, partially worn smooth by time. She reached the podium and placed the box gently atop it.

A click.

They all froze.

The light shifted. A subtle lens effect passed through the thin slit above, throwing a triangular halo across the altar. Sarah instinctively reached toward the glyph beneath the box — the same ringed crest from her father's journal — when suddenly…

A breath of wind.

The wrong kind.

She turned—

—and the world detonated.

From beyond the outer corridor came the sharp crack of suppressed gunfire. Not warning shots. Not intimidation.

Kill shots.

Stone erupted beside her as bullets chewed into the far wall. The beam of light shattered into dust as something heavy slammed against the dome above, showering the space in stone fragments.

Jack was already moving. "**Contact!**" he bellowed, diving in from the corridor and dragging Sarah down behind the low altar just as another volley tore through where she'd been standing.

Victor, who had posted himself near the entrance, rolled behind a fractured column and returned fire with tight, precise bursts.

"Three on the ridge! More coming low!" he called out.

Nora was already in motion, ducking behind a fallen slab along the left wall, drawing her pistol mid-dive and firing into the shadows without hesitation.

"They flanked us!" she snarled. **"How the hell did they get that close?"**

Sarah lay curled beside the podium, breath shallow, one arm protectively over the box.

Then came the shadows.

Six — maybe seven — masked figures, cloaked in black and moving with military precision. No insignias. No markings. Just hardened motion and ruthless efficiency.

The Order.

"Suppress left!" Jack barked. **"Victor, shift cover!"**

Victor grinned behind gritted teeth. "Let's make 'em regret walking through that door."

A roar of return fire shook the crypt.

From deeper inside the adjoining tunnel, Harper appeared — limping but alert — weapon raised and breathing hard. **"Two on the flank. One with support gear. Might be guiding the others."**

Jack nodded. "**Push them back. We're not boxed in. Not yet.**"

The team moved like gears in an old watch, each piece knowing the other's place.

But Sarah felt none of it.

She pressed her back against the cold podium, her fingers gripping the edge of the box, her heartbeat deafening in her ears. She didn't know whether the trap had just been physical — or something worse.

Because the lock hadn't responded.

But the box had.

And that whisper…

…it hadn't come from the wind.

The Interrogation

The safehouse smelled like dust and oil — like time had folded inward and left only sweat and memory behind. Its concrete walls, sun-bleached and thick, muffled the distant chaos of the world outside. Inside, the heat was heavy but survivable.

The surviving Order soldier was bound to an iron support post in one of the back rooms. Duct tape across the mouth, zip cuffs at the wrists and ankles, a blindfold over bloodied eyes. He sat slumped but alert — breathing shallow, chin tilted like he was already somewhere else in his mind.

Harper stood a few feet away, arms crossed, shoulder braced against the wall. He watched the man for a long moment before pulling a folding chair across the dusty floor and sitting down with a grunt.

"You ever been to Volgograd?" Harper asked, voice casual, conversational.

No answer, of course.

He leaned forward, elbows on his knees. “I had a guy there once, told me every prisoner has three tells: the twitch, the blink, and the pause. He was right more often than not. So let’s play a game. I talk. You stay quiet. Let’s see what gives you away.”

Jack leaned against the doorframe, arms crossed, silent. Sarah stood further back, arms wrapped tight around herself, still carrying the weight of the last few hours. Victor watched from the hallway, listening more than observing, one eye on Nora, who hadn’t said a word since they arrived.

Harper pulled the tape free — slowly. The prisoner didn’t flinch. His lips cracked as they parted, dry from heat and silence.

“You’re wasting time,” the man croaked. His accent was faint — Eastern European, masked beneath practiced English. “I’m trained. You know that.”

Harper gave a slow smile. "Oh, I know. But you're also human. You bleed. You breathe. You crack."

"You won't break me."

"I'm not here to break you," Harper said. "I'm here to listen."

Silence.

Harper continued. "You came in hot and fast. You knew the layout of that crypt better than anyone should. You had formations, angles, fallback routes. So… either you've been here before, or someone fed you the blueprint. Which is it?"

The prisoner said nothing.

Harper let the pause stretch. Then: "There's a leak. Maybe local, maybe not. But someone's feeding you intel."

A flicker — tiny. A shift in jaw muscle. Harper clocked it.

Jack stepped forward. "Was it satellite feed? Drone trace? Or do you have a mole watching our movements?"

"Maybe one of you is talking," the prisoner said, smiling through cracked lips. "Maybe someone close."

That got a reaction. Nora's eyes flicked to the side — just enough for Victor to catch it. Jack didn't move.

Harper tilted his head. "Funny thing about lies. Even when they're true, no one believes them until it's too late."

The prisoner grinned. "You won't stop it. It's already begun."

"Stop what?"

"The return."

Harper leaned in. "That mean something to you, or are you just reciting lines like a good little fanatic?"

No answer.

The grin faded.

Sarah stepped forward, voice quiet. "What were you doing at the crypt? What did you expect to find?"

"We were watching. Waiting for something to open. For someone to open it." His gaze settled vaguely in Sarah's direction.

Jack stiffened.

Harper's tone darkened. "You weren't supposed to engage?"

"We were supposed to confirm."

"Confirm what?"

Another grin — this one colder. "That the Guardian had awakened."

Silence spread through the room like a fresh wound.

Harper stood slowly. "That's enough."

"I'll die before I tell you anything else," the man said, voice thin. "But I won't die here. Not by your hand."

Harper raised an eyebrow. "You sure about that?"

The prisoner bit down hard.

For a second, nothing happened.

Then his body seized.

Harper lunged, but it was too late — blood at the lips, a rattling breath, and the eyes rolled back.

"Cyanide capsule," Jack muttered. "Back molar."

Harper stood over the body, jaw tight. "Damn it."

Victor stepped in from the hallway. "We'll bag him. Get him on ice and out of here. Maybe someone topside can still pull something."

"Maybe," Harper muttered.

Sarah didn't say a word. She looked at Jack, then at Nora.

And for the first time since all this began, the silence between them no longer felt safe.

Sarah's Internal Reflection — Guardian Awakening

Sarah stood frozen, staring at the lifeless man on the floor.

"The Guardian has awakened."

The words clung to her ribs like something alive, something buried and now twitching beneath her skin.

She'd seen the term before — not in one place, but many. Scattered through the glyphs lining the cave walls, mentioned cryptically in her father's journal, whispered through the star map's radiance, and once — in a dream too vivid to ignore — spoken without words by a presence cloaked in warmth and calm.

Guardian.

The term hadn't made sense at first. Not really. It sounded ceremonial. Hollow. But now, staring at the corpse of a man who had come to die simply to confirm her existence, it didn't feel hollow at all.

She turned inward.

Pieces surfaced.

In the language of the stone — this living, shifting script that had begun to unravel beneath her fingertips — three titles repeated with weighted significance:

Steward. Sanctari. Guardian.

The **Steward**, as her father's notes described in hushed, reverent tone, was the original keeper. Chosen when the Stone was first hidden — more historian than warrior. A protector of memory, not muscle. And always apart. Distant. Watching from the edge of the story.

The **Sanctari** was different — not chosen through bloodline, but drawn by resilience, conviction, and an unspoken bond to justice. They were the sword. The flame. Defenders of the one who must not fall. And somehow… Jack fit that silhouette more with each step they took.

But the **Guardian**…

Her breath caught.

The Guardian was not trained. Not raised in secret. The Guardian was *called.*

They were born into it — unaware — until something shifted. A lock. A dream. A whisper. The moment wasn't always grand. Sometimes, it was as quiet as touching a stone at sunset.

But when the call came, everything began to change.

Sarah looked down at her hands. She had translated glyphs she'd never studied. Walked paths that didn't exist on maps. She had *felt* places before she saw them. Solved riddles that spoke in metaphors only she seemed to understand.

Not because she was brilliant.

But because something inside her already *knew*.

She had never claimed to be a believer. Not in destiny. Not in fate. But this…

This wasn't belief.

It was **recognition**.

And the enemy had seen it before she had.

"The Guardian has awakened."

Sarah closed her eyes, just for a breath, and let the title settle on her like dust in sunlight.

She didn't speak.

Not yet.

But in her heart, something ancient had just turned over and opened its eyes.

The Unspoken Realization

The fire crackled softly in the safehouse courtyard. The battle was over, but the air still held its breath.

Jack stood apart from the others, leaning against a stone pillar worn smooth by time and weather. His rifle rested against the wall behind him, forgotten. His eyes weren't on the door or the tree line. They were fixed on Sarah.

She sat alone on a low bench near the fire, her back to the flames, silhouetted by their flickering light. Her shoulders had gone still — too still — the kind of stillness that only followed revelation. Jack didn't need to hear her speak to know something had changed.

He'd seen it happen in the cave, at the plateau, in the way she'd stepped into places she couldn't explain with maps. But here, now… it wasn't just instinct.

Something had awakened in her.

He felt it.

Not like heat or light. Not even like intuition. More like gravity. A silent pull that told him she was now the center of whatever storm they were walking into — and that he was no longer just here to keep her alive.

He was here because he couldn't not be.

Jack shifted his weight, uncertain. He didn't know what any of this meant. Not really. But the way she had looked when that man from the Order called her the Guardian — it rattled him. She hadn't flinched. She had absorbed it. Like the word fit in a space inside her that had always been waiting.

He wasn't good at this part — the part where emotions moved quieter than bullets and orders. But something was forming in his chest. Not the kind of protection he was assigned to give. Not the kind that ended when the job did.

This was deeper.

And it scared the hell out of him.

Across the room, Nora watched them both from the shadows near the archway. She didn't move, didn't blink.

She had heard the words, too.

"The Guardian has awakened."

It should have been confirmation — validation of what she'd told the Order, what she had suspected since the moment she saw Sarah deciphering symbols no one else could see. But seeing it now, here, up close…

It was something else entirely.

The others hadn't noticed it yet — not fully. But Nora had been trained to spot subtle shifts. Patterns. Power. Sarah had crossed an invisible line, and the ripple was already spreading.

Nora felt it in her bones.

And it chilled her more than it should have.

Because she hadn't planned on caring. She hadn't planned on being part of this for real. But watching Sarah now — the calm in her posture, the silence in her hands — made Nora realize something terrifying:

She believed in her.

And that belief… it could get them all killed.

So she slipped away before anyone noticed, retreating into the corner of the old stone room, where her shadows still felt like armor.

She would report what she had to.

Nothing more.

But as she turned her back on the firelight, she whispered under her breath — too quiet for anyone but herself:

"You're not supposed to matter."

And yet… she did.

Rerouted

Dawn came quietly.

No radiant fanfare. No grand display of color. Just a soft shift — cool light easing into the shadows of the safehouse, stretching across the flagstones like a hand reaching for a forgotten book.

Jack was already up.

He sat at the old wooden table in the main room, nursing a mug of something that passed for coffee. The map was spread out before him — the one Sarah had been marking with every lock, every shift in instinct, every clue.

But today, it was Sarah who leaned over it.

Her finger hovered above a point in the southern quadrant — nothing but barren ridges and fractured foothills according to satellite imagery. But something tugged at her gut every time she looked at it.

"It doesn't look like anything," Jack said quietly.

"I know."

"Which means it probably is."

She glanced at him. There was a hint of amusement there, buried beneath the tired lines at the corners of his eyes. A shared rhythm, forged through friction.

"Something about this place feels… wrong," she admitted. "Not dangerous. Just… misaligned. Like it's wearing a mask."

Jack folded his arms. "Same way you felt heading toward the false crypt?"

She nodded. "Only backward. That place called to me even though it was wrong. This one doesn't call at all. But it's pulling something else." She tapped the spot again. "The box hasn't responded since the plateau, but this… this might be what the last symbols were pointing to."

Victor entered then, brushing dirt from his sleeves. "Took a walk. Had to make sure no one was camping the perimeter. We're clear."

Jack didn't look up. "Any movement?"

"None. Whoever's left is lying low. Or licking wounds."

Sarah pointed again. "We're heading here."

Victor studied it. "What's there?"

"Nothing," Sarah said. "Which is what makes it interesting."

"Nothing is hard to guard," Victor muttered. "Harder to breach. Could be a vault. Or worse."

Nora stepped in last, her eyes scanning the room before they settled on the map.

She said nothing.

But Jack watched her carefully.

"We move in an hour," he said. "Pack light. Full gear. Expect contact, even if there isn't any."

No one argued.

They moved.

On the trail

They hiked in silence, the path winding through fractured earth and wind-swept rock. Sarah walked ahead of the group, as if something invisible was guiding her feet. The terrain grew more unstable the closer they got — hairline cracks in the shale, strange dips in elevation that didn't match the topography.

Jack watched her carefully. He'd noticed it before — the way she moved faster the closer she got to something real. Like her body already knew the route even if her mind hadn't caught up.

"You okay?" he asked when they paused for water.

She looked at him, unsure for a moment what he meant.

Then: "Yeah. Just… I had a dream."

Jack waited.

"I think it was the entity," she continued. "The good one. The one I felt before the plateau. It told me… whatever path I choose, if I trust the instinct, I won't lose it."

He was quiet for a beat.

"That's vague as hell," he said finally.

She smiled faintly. "Welcome to my world."

He smirked, but his eyes didn't leave hers. "Still trust it?"

"I don't have a choice. I think I'm supposed to."

Jack looked away. But he said, just loud enough for her to hear, "I trust you."

It hit her harder than she expected.

Not because of the words — but because of the way he said them.

Quiet. Final. Like something he hadn't admitted even to himself.

They walked on.

The Ambush and the Flight

They approached the ridge just before mid-afternoon.

The trail had narrowed into a blind curve framed by sandstone cliffs and scrub, forcing them to move single file. The terrain was too tight for the drone to get a wide sweep, and Jack didn't like it.

"Victor," he said quietly, "take flank. Nora, keep Sarah between us. Eyes wide."

Victor grunted acknowledgment, slipping off the trail to the right and disappearing into the boulders. Jack felt the familiar tension creep down his spine — the kind that had nothing to do with fear and everything to do with instinct.

Sarah, for her part, was distracted.

The box in her pack had started to vibrate again.

Not enough to be visible. Just a faint rhythm, like a second heartbeat ticking from between her shoulder blades. She didn't mention it. Not yet.

Because then the world cracked open.

A burst echoed from the ridge above — followed by the sharp hiss of smoke and the snap of something slicing the air.

"Contact!" Jack shouted, spinning on instinct as a burst of automatic fire ripped down across the trail.

Sarah dropped instantly, Jack over her in one motion, shielding her with his body behind an outcrop. Victor returned fire from the flank, forcing the shooters to duck. Nora disappeared — no order needed — her pistol already drawn as she slipped into the rocks, flanking left.

Three assailants moved down from the ridge — armored in desert-camouflage gear with visors that reflected light like oil-slicks. No insignia. But Jack had seen that posture before. The discipline. The formation.

Arcane Order.

He gritted his teeth.

So it's real.

He fired twice, pinning one of the gunmen behind a jut of stone.

"Victor!" he shouted. "Three on high ground. Keep them split."

Victor fired a smoke canister toward the ridge. It exploded in a wall of white. Jack pulled Sarah to her feet.

"We're moving."

They sprinted low across the trail, bullets stitching the rocks behind them. Sarah didn't hesitate — didn't stumble. It was like her body knew where not to step.

Jack slammed his shoulder into a side path that dipped between the rocks, clearing a route. "Nora!"

"I see them!" she shouted from above, discharging two shots with deadly accuracy. One of the gunmen screamed — then went silent.

Then it turned.

One of the attackers broke formation and made a run for the opposite slope.

Jack raised his weapon — hesitated — then fired low.

The man dropped with a broken leg, howling in pain.

Another gunman lunged toward Sarah.

Jack turned—

—but Victor was faster. He slammed the attacker into the wall with the butt of his rifle. The man fell, dazed but alive.

Two were down. One was dead. And the runner—

Jack turned back.

Gone.

Damn it.

They regrouped fast.

Victor knelt beside the still-breathing attacker and zip-tied his hands. "One's dead. One ran. This one's lucky."

Jack searched the pockets, swept the gear — nothing traceable. Standard black-market modifications, tactical redundancies, zero ID.

But the eyes… cold. Focused.

Not militia. Not mercs.

Order.

Nora dropped beside them, her face blank.

"They knew we'd be here," Jack muttered. "This wasn't random."

Victor nodded grimly. "Positioned for a crossfire. But not well. Rushed."

Jack looked over at the injured prisoner, already shifting like he knew what was coming.

"We interrogate him," Harper said as he approached from below. He'd been trailing quietly since they broke camp, letting them move forward while he monitored for pursuit.

Jack didn't question his appearance — not now.

Harper knelt beside the attacker and looked him in the eyes.

"Let's have a talk."

Cutaway – Interrogation, Moments Later

They dragged the prisoner into the shade beneath the overhang. Blood seeped from a shallow graze at his temple, but his eyes were sharp. Too sharp.

Harper crouched in front of him.

"You're not going to talk," he said. "That's fine. But you will listen."

No response.

"You were sent here. You knew we'd be here. That means someone fed you the intel — or you've been watching us for longer than we thought."

The prisoner smirked. "You're smarter than the others."

"I'm older than the others."

Nothing.

Then Harper leaned in, voice low. "Who told you where we'd be?"

"Winds change. So do paths."

Harper backhanded him — not hard, just enough to knock the smile off his face.

"Try again."

"I follow orders. I don't ask names."

"You have one job now — stay alive."

A flicker of something behind the man's eyes.

Then: "There's always someone close. Always someone feeding the dark. Maybe it's one of yours."

Jack stepped in. "Is that a guess, or do you know something?"

No answer.

He was baiting them.

But Harper saw it — the tension in his arms. The way he flexed his jaw.

"He's going to try to off himself," Harper warned. "Now."

Victor moved first — injecting a sedative into the man's arm before the capsule in his mouth could crack.

The prisoner slumped.

Alive. Barely.

Victor exhaled. "We need to move him. Keep him isolated. If he wakes, we try again."

Jack looked toward the horizon.

"If they know where we are now, they'll know again. Someone is watching us."

His eyes flicked to Nora — not accusatory, but aware.

She met his gaze. Said nothing.

Sarah stood apart, the box clutched in her hand.

Still glowing.

Still pulling.

Return to Ash and Stone

The air was thick with smoke and sweat as the last of the makeshift bandages were secured and their gear rechecked. They hadn't moved far from the battle site. They couldn't. Not in their current state.

Jack crouched near the edge of the rocky trail, inspecting the scattered debris that had once been their supply bag. Two canisters were split open, one of the medical kits was soaked through, and the water filtration gear was shattered.

He cursed quietly.

"No more forward movement," he muttered.

Behind him, Victor finished zip-tying the prisoner's limbs to a stretch of rigid tarp. The man still hadn't woken — and they preferred it that way for now. Too many questions. Not enough time.

"I'm down to two mags," Victor said. "Harper's at one and a half. We're low on water, communications are glitching, and I think the drone controller's shot."

Nora held up the device with a frown. "Took a hit during the crossfire. Won't hold connection. I'll need time to patch it."

No one questioned her too closely. That had been her intention.

Jack looked to Sarah, whose fingers curled tightly around the box again. The glow had subsided — but the pulse within her hadn't.

"This isn't the spot," she said, quietly. "But we were close."

"I know," Jack replied. "But we can't keep pushing blind. Not now."

Sarah looked at the scorched ridge ahead. Her jaw tightened, disappointment flickering through her expression.

"There was something here," she whispered. "I could feel it. I was close."

"You'll feel it again," Harper said, stepping in beside her. "You just need time to listen."

Victor nodded toward the canyon mouth. "We fall back. The safehouse is still closer than any settlement. We regroup, resupply, interrogate when the bastard wakes. And I call in a backup route for us."

Sarah didn't argue.

Not because she agreed.

But because she knew Jack was right. Harper was right. The next step couldn't be rushed.

Even the Stone didn't move in straight lines.

They moved by dusk.

Victor and Harper carried the prisoner between them, his unconscious form swaying with each step. Jack led the front, weapon high, constantly scanning. Nora brought up the rear, silent — thoughtful — clutching the damaged drone controller in her bag.

Because the Order was getting aggressive.

Too aggressive.

And if they were willing to risk this much, something bigger had changed.

She needed answers. Fast. Even if it meant contacting a handler she hadn't spoken to in weeks.

Her cover was threadbare.

And now, worse than being outed — she wasn't sure whose side she was still on.

Chapter Six: The Whispered Stone

The Dream of Duality

The night was too quiet.

Even within the walls of the safe house — thick stone, reinforced doors, buried beneath layers of earth and secrecy — Sarah couldn't sleep. Her body was exhausted, her muscles sore from battle and retreat, but her mind hummed like a struck chord.

Eventually, sleep claimed her.

But peace did not.

She stood in a vast, starlit field — the sky above her neither night nor day, but something in between, humming with pale light that didn't cast shadows. The ground was soft and dusted with ash, yet her feet left no prints.

In the distance, something shimmered.

She turned — and the horizon cracked open like glass.

From the fracture came two figures.

One was cloaked in warmth. Not radiant, not blinding — just *present.* Its shape shimmered, genderless and calm, made of woven strands of memory and wind. Where it walked, ancient symbols followed, blooming like petals in the air.

The other came behind.

A silhouette darker than the space it stepped through. It didn't walk — it *bent* the world. No footsteps, no sound. Its presence was a weight. A hunger. A pressure that pulled light inward and left silence trembling in its wake.

The first spoke, though its mouth did not move.

"You are the first to hear. The Guardian has awakened."

Sarah opened her mouth, but no sound came.

The figure continued:

"Time folds. The Order closes in. They believe they seek power. They do not know what walks behind them."

The dark shape loomed larger now, indistinct but watching. The air around it hissed, not in sound — but in memory. Like flame devouring parchment. Like trust betrayed.

Sarah took a step backward.

"What is it?" she tried to say. The thought barely escaped.

The warm figure answered, not in words, but in images:
— The Stone glowing in a cradle of bone-white rock.
— A child reaching for it.
— Fire erupting.
— A sky torn open.
— Voices crying out as if the earth itself had split.

Then words again:

"Vel'takar. The Loosed Flame. Born when the Stone was first misused. Bound by its will. Hungry for its release."

The dark presence pulsed once — and Sarah felt heat behind her eyes, as if her bones remembered something her mind could not.

"Why me?" she whispered.

The warm entity reached out. A single glyph appeared between them, spinning slowly. The symbol of the Guardian.

"You are not the first. But you are the first in this time. The first to awaken when the Stone is near its choosing."

Behind her, the darkness moved — closer, impatient.

"The Order seeks access. They cannot reach it without one like you. That is why you were

brought together. That is why the Sanctari was called. Why the Steward watched."

Sarah's breath caught. Jack. Harper. Her father.

Everything had been converging, even when she hadn't known it.

"What do I do?" she asked.

The glyph faded. The ground beneath her cracked slightly, and from it rose a final image:

The Stone — pulsing. Vibrating. As if trying to speak.

And then, the words:

"Trust what speaks from within. What follows light may be shadow. What hides in silence may be truth."

She awoke with a gasp.

Sweat clung to her back. Her hands trembled. The walls of the safe house were unchanged — dim, silent, solid.

But the dream still pulsed behind her ribs.

Sarah sat up, rubbing the side of her neck, and reached for the notebook at her bedside. Her pencil moved before her thoughts caught up — sketching the glyph, the Stone, the crack in the earth.

And finally, a name she hadn't heard aloud but now knew by heart.

Vel'takar.

The Loosed Flame was watching.

And the race to reach the Stone had just become something far more terrifying than a secret war.

Strategic Reckoning

Safehouse – Early Morning, Post-Battle

The battered quiet of the safehouse settled like smoke.

Wind brushed against the broken shutters, stirring the scent of desert grit and old canvas. Inside, the team moved with the stillness of exhaustion—each carrying bruises, smoke-stained gear, and the weight of things they hadn't said yet.

Victor leaned over a table in the center of the main room, a worn topographical map stretched flat beneath his hands. One sleeve was rolled past a gash on his arm, field-dressed with practiced speed. His expression was calm, but the tension in his shoulders betrayed calculation beneath the surface.

Jack stood beside him, arms crossed, a half-empty canteen dangling from one hand. He hadn't said much since the retreat, but his silence had a rhythm—watching. Measuring.

Harper limped in from the hallway, a strip of cloth tucked beneath his arm like a sling and a battered pistol holstered at his side. "Anyone figure out how the hell they knew where to hit us?"

Victor didn't look up. "Working theory? They've been monitoring this region longer than we thought. Could be long-range recon. Could be something worse."

Nora, seated near the far window, sharpened a blade methodically on a whetstone. She didn't flinch.

Jack glanced over at her. "You didn't look surprised when they showed up."

"Wasn't," she said flatly. "Figured someone would eventually come looking."

Harper's eyes narrowed, but he said nothing. Not yet.

Sarah entered, wiping dust from her palms with a cloth. She looked tired, but alert — like her thoughts had outrun her body. "They weren't just searching. They were waiting."

Victor tapped a spot on the map. "This crypt wasn't random. They believed it was a valid location — likely acting on old intelligence. That means we're not the only ones chasing riddles."

Jack leaned in. "Which brings us to a new problem. If they've got partial maps, copied glyphs, any of that, they could be chasing the same trail we are."

"Or trying to corrupt it," Sarah added.

Victor nodded. "Either way — they're catching up."

A long silence fell over the group. Dust swirled between floorboards. Somewhere outside, a bird called, sharp and solitary.

Jack broke the quiet. "So. What now?"

Victor stepped back from the map, pulling a folded paper from his vest. It was a satellite composite — older, grainy — with several markings scrawled in red ink.

"We adjust. We plan. We move."

He tapped a point along a crescent-shaped ridge near the bottom edge of the map. "There's a site here. Old survey teams ignored it. No artifacts, no visible ruins. But I had a local contact years ago who swore by it — said the place felt wrong."

"Wrong?" Harper asked.

"Quiet in a way that didn't sit right. No echo. No wildlife. Like the land was holding its breath."

Sarah stepped closer. "A null zone?"

"Maybe," Victor said. "But that's not all."

He pulled the Order captive's satchel from under the table and dumped it out. Among the contents: a cracked comm unit, blood-streaked gloves, and a notebook filled with loose sketches and location names.

Victor turned to a page marked by a simple phrase, circled three times:

"Sanctuary echo?"

Jack's brows lifted slightly. "You think it's the next site?"

"I think it's the one they couldn't open."

Everyone looked at Sarah.

She blinked. "I'd need more—"

"Not more," Victor interrupted gently. "You. You're the difference. The reason they're tracking us instead of digging on their own."

Sarah didn't answer.

Harper stepped forward, nodding toward the page. "Then we need to hit it before they regroup."

Nora said nothing. But her hand paused on the whetstone.

Victor looked to Jack. "You know the terrain better than most. You think we can move through the ridge undetected?"

Jack's gaze drifted to Sarah. "We'll manage."

Sarah finally spoke, her voice low. "This next one… I don't feel it yet. Not like the others."

Victor tilted his head. "Then maybe it hasn't called. Or maybe it's waiting to see if you still trust yourself."

She met his eyes. "I do."

But her tone carried a hint of doubt — the kind that comes only after something ancient whispers your name.

Quiet Interlude – Beneath the Noise

The safehouse had quieted.

Most of the others were resting or cleaning gear, the crackle of Victor's shortwave radio drifting faintly from the next room. Outside, wind moved across the hills like breath across old skin. But inside, the silence was full — thick with recovery, exhaustion, and thought.

Jack stood near the open doorframe, leaning against it with a cup of lukewarm coffee. His shirt was half-buttoned, sleeves rolled up, eyes set somewhere just beyond the horizon.

Sarah sat on a low bench across the room, hunched over her notebook again. Always writing. Always studying. The stone box rested nearby, half-wrapped in cloth, as if even now it needed protection.

He watched her for a moment longer, then finally spoke.

"You look exhausted."

She didn't look up. "I'm fine."

"You're not," he said, stepping in. "You're bleeding from five scratches, your hand's swollen, and you haven't slept since we got here."

"I'll sleep after we get to the next site."

Jack crouched beside her. "You're an academic, Sarah. This — gunfire, smoke, dragging people out of crypts — it's not your world."

She met his eyes. "It is now."

That hit him harder than it should have.

He looked away, then back again. "You know… I keep trying to figure out how you're still holding together."

"Adrenaline. Stubbornness. Maybe destiny." She smiled faintly.

Jack didn't smile back — not quite. "You ever think maybe you should sit this one out?"

"You ever think maybe I can't?"

Silence stretched between them for a beat. Then Jack, quietly, said, "You scare me."

Sarah blinked. "Excuse me?"

"You're brave as hell," he clarified. "And brilliant. And you walk into darkness like it's your inheritance. That's not normal."

She shrugged. "Neither are glowing symbols or sentient caves. You're the one who said this wasn't a military op."

Jack exhaled, then nodded toward the adjoining room. "That intern of yours. Nora."

Sarah's brows lifted. "What about her?"

Jack leaned against the bench. "She's good. Really good. Too good. I've worked with drone teams, recon outfits, even some private-sector types. And I've never seen someone pivot from ground survey to tactical overwatch as fast as she does."

"She told me she served," Sarah said quickly. "A volunteer corp, maybe intelligence-adjacent. She doesn't talk about it."

"No," Jack said. "She doesn't. That's the thing."

Sarah hesitated, then offered a small shake of her head. "I trust her."

"I don't distrust her," Jack said. "But you and I both know that a quiet past usually means a loud one."

Sarah didn't answer. She glanced toward the other room, where Nora's silhouette passed briefly across the curtain. Then back at Jack.

"You think she's lying?"

"I think," he said carefully, "she's more than she claims to be. And whatever that is — it's worth watching."

He looked back at Sarah then, softer now. "But if you tell me she's safe, I'll take your word. For now."

Sarah gave a faint smile. "I trust her. But I'll watch her."

He nodded, then stood slowly. "Good. Because I don't want to watch you walk into something without someone watching your back."

She reached out, just briefly, and touched his hand as he turned to go. "Thanks for watching."

He looked down at their hands. His thumb brushed hers, just barely.

"Anytime, Professor."

And he left her to the silence.

But not the solitude.

Nora Alone – Fractured Allegiance

The corridor was empty.

Nora stood at the far end of the safehouse near a small, dust-caked window, the moonlight slicing through the slats in pale strips across her face. Her hand rested on the edge of the windowsill, knuckles white.

She wasn't tired — not in the usual way. Her body ached, her ribs still throbbed from the fight, but her mind was alive, fracturing under the weight of too many roles.

Too many masks.

She heard Jack's voice faintly through the wall. Low. Controlled. Probably talking to Sarah. Probably saying something noble and blunt — the kind of thing good men said when they were just starting to realize they were in trouble.

And Sarah… Sarah had changed.

Nora had seen it. Noticed the weight in her voice, the way the air shifted around her when she touched the box, when she spoke about the stone, when she entered the crypt like it belonged to her.

Because maybe it did.

The Guardian has awakened.

She'd reported it — reluctantly. Too much, and they'd pull her. Too little, and they'd send someone less… subtle.

And now there were whispers inside the Order. Not just about the stone, but about her. Field agents weren't supposed to get too close. Weren't supposed to feel anything.

And yet here she was, standing in an abandoned safehouse in a worn tank top and dusty boots, wondering if Jack Thompson was starting to suspect her.

Because he should.

He'd seen too much. Not enough to know the truth — but enough to feel it.

He was dangerous.

And Sarah…

Sarah was more dangerous still.

Because Nora was starting to believe in her.

She reached into her satchel, fingertips brushing the cold metal of the encrypted comm tucked beneath a false seam. She didn't pull it out. Not yet.

But soon.

Soon, they'd want answers. Progress reports. Proof that their investment — their sleeper — was paying off.

And Nora would have to decide if her loyalty still lay with the Order…

…or with the woman who was becoming something greater than any prophecy had dared predict.

Crossed Wires

The safehouse hummed with a kind of unsettled quiet. No fire crackled. No one spoke loudly. The team had split into pairs and corners — patching wounds, reviewing weapons, rehydrating with forced sips from canteens.

But in one dimly lit room, beneath a busted ceiling fan and beside a rust-flaked generator that hadn't run in years, Nora knelt alone with the drone controller open in her lap.

The casing was intact. Superficially.

But a thin panel along the underside had been removed — delicately pried open and rewired. No one would've noticed unless they knew what to look for. Even Jack, with all his suspicion, hadn't had time to examine it closely.

Her fingers moved with precision. Not hesitation.

A soft blue glow lit her face as she activated the hidden frequency. The unit clicked once. Twice. Then a faint tone pulsed — low enough not to travel beyond the cracked stone walls.

"Specter 9 reporting. Encrypted channel only. Immediate read-back required."

Static. Then, a voice. Tinny. Hollow.

"Specter 9, relay."

Nora inhaled slowly. Her tone remained clipped. Professional.

"Guardian confirmed. Third lock compromised. Hostiles engaged. One prisoner retained — Order combatant. Request extraction for intel or transfer orders. Current position... unstable."

There was a long pause.

Then the voice returned, colder than before.

"Confirmed. Maintain cover. Do not deviate from embedded role. Additional teams mobilized. Your presence is still required."

Nora gritted her teeth.

"They're getting suspicious. The Guardian is becoming..." she hesitated, ***"...aware."***

Another pause.

Then, the voice again.

"Proceed with caution. You are not to interfere with the next activation. Observation only. Report again upon arrival."

The signal ended. The soft glow blinked out. Nora sat for a moment in the dark, exhaling through her nose.

She didn't notice Jack's shadow pass by the hallway.

But he noticed the blue flicker.

Same Night — Interrogation Room (Rear of the Safehouse)

The surviving Order operative sat tied to a rusted pipe in the utility room — bruised, dehydrated, but awake.

Harper crouched in front of him, calm but coiled. He held a half-filled bottle of water, casually turning it in his hand.

"You ever work surveillance?" Harper asked, voice dry.

The operative said nothing.

Harper shrugged. "I did. For twenty years. County sheriff's office. Before that, military police. You know what gets people caught?"

The man didn't answer.

"Patterns," Harper continued. "Doesn't matter how deep you hide your trail — people repeat themselves. Habits. Calls. Lies. I've seen murderers who can walk through fire, but they can't change the way they blink when they're lying."

He leaned in closer.

"You blinked wrong back at the ridge. You were watching us long before your friends moved. You knew where to strike."

Still silence.

"Now…" Harper set the water down just out of reach, "…you want to tell me how that's possible?"

The operative licked his lips, eyes half-lidded. "You talk too much."

Harper smiled slightly. "You're not the first to say that."

From the corner, Victor stepped forward. "You've got two options. You can give us something — anything — and maybe we let you live a little longer. Or you can keep dancing, and we hand you over to people who won't ask nicely."

The man finally looked up. "It won't matter. You're already being watched."

Harper's eyes narrowed. "What's that supposed to mean?"

The prisoner gave a hollow smile.

"Someone on your team is feeding intel. Maybe they don't even know it. Maybe they do. Either way, you're late."

Jack stepped in just then, standing behind Harper.

"And you're bleeding out information," he growled. "You want to die, fine. But don't lie on your way out. We've seen what happens when your kind comes to play."

The operative met his eyes, and for just a second, there was something else there — fear?

Then he lunged — head snapping back hard into the wall.

Too late, Harper grabbed for him — but the motion had already triggered something hidden in his mouth.

A crunch.

A gasp.

Then nothing.

The body slumped forward, twitching once. Then stilled.

Victor swore.

Jack shook his head. "They're trained for this."

Harper exhaled through clenched teeth. "I was hoping we'd at least get a trail."

Victor turned to leave. "We got enough. Someone tipped them off. And whoever that is — they're still with us."

While the interrogation buzzed with tension behind rusted doors and low voices, Sarah sat alone in the main room, her back to a broken wall that let in the silver edge of moonlight. The box sat open before her, the inner mechanism still and cold, its once-glowing star map now dormant.

But she wasn't looking at the box.

She was staring at her transcriptions — glyphs copied from the chamber's walls, stacked beside the sketches from her father's journal. Charcoal lines intersected with graphite notes, scattered across maps and weather-worn vellum like an unsolved equation painted by instinct.

Her fingers traced a curve in the margins — a sweep of symbols that had, until now, seemed decorative.

But the shape… it repeated. Subtly. Nested inside itself. Like an arc within an arc.

Her heart slowed.

She flipped back to the map projection the box had displayed on the plateau — the star map. At the time, it had pointed toward the crypt they'd just fled. But she'd assumed it was a fixed alignment. A singular destination.

Now, with the glyphs echoing in her bones, she realized something else:

It wasn't a point. It was a vector.

A celestial arc, yes — but not ending where they thought.

The plateau projection had offered an anchor — a misdirection by design. The true path bent away at an angle only visible in the glyphs she hadn't understood until now.

And that path?

It aimed straight for a valley long thought mythical. A name scribbled in the margins of one of her father's early notebooks. Dismissed even by him as a translation error.

Valis Thaan.

She whispered the name aloud.

The map didn't react, but something in her chest did — a soft tug, familiar now. The resonance.

Jack appeared behind her, silent, arms crossed but unreadable.

"You're not resting," he said quietly.

She didn't look up. "I think the crypt was a decoy."

His brow furrowed. "You're sure?"

She finally glanced over her shoulder. "The alignment was wrong. The pull… it wasn't there. I wanted it to be. But the glyphs were meant to redirect. Not just mislead an enemy — test a Guardian."

Jack took a slow breath. "That valley you're pointing to…"

"You know it?" she asked.

Victor's voice came from the corner — he'd entered silently, dirt still on his boots from patrol.

"I've only heard the name whispered once," he said. "Most think it's just a legend. A dead end."

Sarah stood slowly. "It's not. My father marked it years ago — before he stopped writing about the Stone. It wasn't just a myth. He didn't go… because something warned him away."

Victor gave her a long look. "Then that's where we go."

The Next Bearing

The safehouse was still. Only the ticking of an old, cracked wall clock and the occasional creak of aging wood filled the silence.

Sarah stood at the center of the main room, maps and notebooks spread across the rickety dining table. Jack leaned against the far wall, arms folded, watching her with the same quiet gravity he'd carried since they first met. Victor sat on an overturned crate, sharpening a field knife with slow, deliberate strokes.

Nora, expression unreadable, stood in the corner, her hands behind her back — too still.

The others had returned from tending gear and wounds. The unspoken weight of the earlier ambush clung to them like smoke.

Sarah placed her hand flat on the map. "The crypt was never the destination. It was designed to mislead, to trap."

Jack's voice was low. "You're sure of that?"

"Yes," she said, glancing at the glyphs beside the star map. "This isn't about where we went. It's about where we go next. A location hidden inside a misaligned path. A place my father once circled in the margins."

She underlined the name with her finger: Valis Thaan.

Victor raised an eyebrow. "You're serious?"

"I'm certain," she said.

"And we're trusting a place no one's seen in decades — if ever — based on a myth," Jack added, but there was no accusation in his tone. Just calculation.

Sarah looked up. "It's not just a myth. The map pointed there. So did the glyphs. And… I feel it. The same way I felt the plateau. The cave."

Jack's eyes stayed on her a moment longer than necessary. Then he nodded.

"Then we prep at first light."

Victor tucked the knife away. "It's a hard route. I'll mark two possible access points. No satellite coverage in the basin — terrain's too steep. But we'll go light and fast."

"We'll move separate from the drone," Jack added. "Use it for scouting only. Nora?"

She nodded. "I'll configure silent sweep patterns. Low altitude."

Sarah didn't miss the hesitation in Nora's voice. It was subtle — but it was there.

No one spoke for a moment.

Then Jack pushed off the wall. "We've lost time. And we've drawn attention."
Victor looked between them. "So we keep moving. Eyes open. Weapons loaded."

Sarah closed the notebook, tucking it under her arm. "We go silent. No transmissions. No unnecessary contact."

Nora gave a faint nod, gaze flicking briefly to Sarah — then to the door.

Jack crossed the room and rested his hand briefly on Sarah's shoulder — not command, not comfort. Just connection.

"Let's finish what we started," he said.

And the room, fractured just hours before, felt — for one breath — united.

Outside, the wind picked up again.

Morning wasn't far.

And in the heart of Valis Thaan, the next lock waited

Chapter Seven: Into the Valley of Echoes

The Journey Begins

They left the safehouse at first light.

No words. Just packed gear, the crunch of boots on gravel, and the occasional mechanical whine as Nora calibrated the drone's onboard stabilizers. The sunrise painted the landscape in rust and brass, but the light felt thin — stretched over something ancient and waiting.

The valley loomed in the distance, visible only as a long, unnatural dip in the earth — a slash where vegetation hesitated and even birds didn't fly overhead. It was quiet. Too quiet.

Sarah sat in the back of the modified utility truck, legs drawn up, notebook open across her thighs. She didn't write. Just stared at the brittle, tea-colored pages her father once filled. Her fingers hovered over a particular scrawled phrase: *"Echoes follow the true path, but only when silence is broken."*

She'd read it a dozen times. Today it rang differently. Today it felt like a warning.

Jack drove the lead vehicle. Eyes forward. Hands loose on the wheel. He wasn't talking much — hadn't since they left. He was watching the terrain with the kind of measured caution that came from experience and something deeper. He couldn't name it, but the tension in his chest hadn't lifted since the battle.

Something about this next step felt… exposed.

"You sure this is the place?" he asked, not turning.

Sarah looked up. "It's not a place I found in the star map. Not directly. But the symbols… once I translated them against my father's notes, this valley kept surfacing. Like a ghost in the text. Quiet, but present."

Jack nodded once. "Victor thinks so too. Said locals call it cursed. No one goes in unless they have to."

"Do we have to?" she asked.

He met her eyes briefly in the mirror. "Yeah. We do."

Behind them, Victor manned the second vehicle, keeping a watchful eye on the perimeter while giving Harper room to rest. The older man sat with his leg braced, still nursing the gunshot wound. But his mind was sharp — too sharp to sit idle.

"This place give you the creeps?" Harper muttered.

Victor gave a slow nod. "Places with no history written down always do."

Nora rode silently in the rear cab with her gear. Her fingers drummed idly on her drone controller, but her mind was elsewhere — on the message that still hadn't come. She'd sent her last encrypted signal two nights ago. Silence ever since.

The Order wasn't responding.

Worse, she wasn't sure if they were watching… or simply done with her.

She felt it like static in her teeth — something between panic and betrayal. If her usefulness was ending, so was her protection.

They crested a ridge and the valley sprawled before them. The road, what was left of it, dipped sharply into a basin choked with twisted rock formations and scrub brush that had long given up trying to survive. The only sound was the wind, and even it was tentative — like the air didn't want to wake whatever lay below.

Sarah leaned forward. "It's different here."

Jack kept one hand on the wheel. "You feel it?"

"Yes. Not like before. It's… quieter."

He scanned the shadows that spilled from the stone columns. "Too quiet."

Sarah nodded slowly. "It's like something's listening."

They reached the edge of the descent and stopped. Beyond it, the earth fell away into steep ravines and folded stone — natural geography twisted by time or something else. And nestled at the far end, nearly swallowed by the cliffside, was a structure. Faint. Worn. But unmistakably *placed.*

Sarah's breath caught.

"That's it."

Jack narrowed his eyes. "Doesn't look welcoming."

Victor's voice crackled over comms. "Never does."

They climbed out, leaving the vehicles behind. From here on, it was by foot.

As the group began to descend into the valley, the sun dipped behind a high ridge — and the wind fell completely still.

Behind them, the last echo of footfalls faded too quickly.

Ahead, the stone waited.

Arrival at the Forgotten Threshold

The path narrowed into a series of craggy switchbacks, carved into the cliff by erosion or ancient hands—it was impossible to tell. The air thickened as they moved deeper into the basin, not in heat or humidity, but in pressure. Like the weight of time pressed against their skin with every step.

The wind never returned.

Sarah felt the silence like a hum behind her ears. She clutched her father's notebook tighter, her other hand brushing the box in her satchel — the one that had led them here. It hadn't pulsed since the last site. But now, just faintly, she could feel warmth again.

As if it too recognized the place.

The stone structure came into view through a gap in the jagged ridge — not massive, but ancient. A squat monument of interlocking blocks so weathered it nearly disappeared into the canyon wall. Its entrance was a black slash across the face, no wider than a single person. The surrounding rock bore no markings, no symbols. Just age.

Jack motioned them to stop, scanning the surroundings with a practiced eye. He gestured to Victor, who took a long, slow arc around the perimeter.

"No prints," Victor said after a moment. "No recent tracks. No movement."

"Too clean," Jack muttered.

Nora lowered her pack and sent the drone forward. It floated silently through the narrow opening and into the darkness. The feed was grainy but functional.

Inside: nothing.

A single chamber. Stone walls. No apparent exits. No signs of tampering or recent disturbance.

Just… stillness.

Sarah stood at the entrance, her brow furrowed. "It's not just a monument. It's a container. But not for something physical. It's holding memory."

Jack gave her a look. "Care to translate that into something we can shoot if needed?"

She almost smiled. "It's old. Older than the maps, older than language. But it's tied to the Stone. I know it."

Victor grunted. "Looks like a tomb to me."

Sarah's voice dropped. "Maybe. But whose?"

They stepped inside one by one, their footsteps echoing hollow and flat. The interior was just as the drone showed — a chamber no bigger than a medium-sized room, circular, with walls covered in a smooth, uninterrupted surface. It felt… deliberate.

And empty.

At first.

Sarah approached the far wall and ran her hand over it. The stone was cool, too smooth for weather. She placed the notebook flat against the surface, comparing the glyphs etched faintly into its pages with the blank wall.

That's when she saw it.

A shimmer. Just below eye level. Only visible from a particular angle. She shifted her position — and there, faint, and ghostlike, a spiral of symbols unfurled across the wall. Not carved. Not painted. *Projected.* By what, she didn't know. But only she could see them.

"The wall's reacting," she whispered. "To me."

Nora stepped closer. "There's nothing there."

"I see it," Sarah said, breathless.

She reached out, not touching, just tracing the air in front of the ghostly text. The glyphs responded, flickering faintly, realigning in a slow cascade until a phrase formed in her mind — not written in words, but felt as thought.

"The Guardian has chosen poorly before."

Her hand trembled. Another line shimmered into view:

"Do not follow echoes that do not ring true."

Behind her, Jack stepped forward. "You okay?"

Sarah swallowed. "I think… this is the place we weren't supposed to come."

Jack's voice lowered. "You saying this is another false site?"

She nodded slowly. "I didn't feel it at first. But now… it's like standing inside someone else's memory. And it doesn't belong to me."

Jack glanced at Victor, who had gone quiet, staring at the wall with something between suspicion and awe.

"Then we leave?" he asked.

Sarah hesitated. "Soon. I want to see what it's willing to show me. If this is a warning, I need to understand it."

Outside, the sky had dimmed with fast-moving clouds that hadn't existed moments before.

Inside, Sarah stepped closer to the wall — and whispered softly, the way she had on the plateau.

The glyphs shimmered again.

And behind them, something moved.

Shadows in Stone

The glyphs recoiled.

That was the only word Sarah could find to describe it — not faded or vanished, but recoiled, like a living thing retreating from light. One moment they were suspended in shimmering arcs across the wall, and the next, they collapsed inward. The chamber dimmed.

Jack instinctively stepped closer, placing himself just behind Sarah's shoulder. His hand drifted near his holster — not drawing yet, but ready. Victor stiffened beside the entrance, gaze sharpening. Nora moved back half a step, eyes narrowing at the shift in energy, calculating the unseen threat.

Then the wall pulsed.

Not light.

Sound.

A low thrum echoed through the stone — deep, resonant, and not entirely… external. It settled into their bones like a second heartbeat. Sarah swayed slightly, steadying herself on the podium-shaped rise at the room's center. Her palm landed flat.

The thrum stopped.

A new pattern appeared.

This time, not in glyphs — but in shadow.

Across the wall, rising as if born from the stone's own memory, a silhouette formed. Humanoid. Not detailed. No face. Just the impression of a figure, cloaked in what looked like smoke and time, its edges constantly unraveling and re-forming.

And a voice.

It came not from the figure, but from *everywhere.*

Low. Measured. Malevolent not in pitch, but in **purpose**.

"She walks the path."

Sarah's breath caught.

Jack stepped in front of her.

"Who's there?" he snapped.

No answer.

The shadow twitched, shifting slightly — and behind it, on the wall, symbols unfurled again. This time Sarah *couldn't* read them. They blurred at the edge of her comprehension, foreign even to her.

Only one word surfaced in her mind:

Vel'takar.

It came with an image. Fire in a circle. Eyes turned black. A hand reaching from beneath a world split in half.

She stumbled backward.

"Sarah?" Jack caught her arm.

She looked up at him, dazed. "It's him. The one… behind everything."

Jack's jaw tightened. "The Order?"

"No. They serve something they don't understand. This is the thing behind it."

Victor was already scanning the walls again, rifle raised. "What thing?"

Nora's voice was soft. Too soft. "Vel'takar."

All heads turned to her.

Jack narrowed his eyes. "You know that name?"

Nora hesitated too long. "Only rumors. From suppressed texts. But yes. If this site's revealing it now… we need to move. This place isn't neutral."

The figure on the wall didn't move. It didn't threaten. It just *was.*

Watching.

Waiting.

Sarah turned back to the glyphs — and they had stilled into one final message. She felt it more than read it.

"Do not bring the flame to the veil."

And then it vanished.

The light. The presence. The shadow.

Gone.

Outside, the wind had returned. Whipping through the cliffs as if trying to fill the silence the thing had left behind.

They stood there in silence for a long moment, until Victor finally broke it.

"That thing we just saw… You're sure that wasn't a recording?"

Sarah shook her head. "It wasn't meant to be seen by anyone not tied to the Stone. It only responded to me."

Jack exhaled slowly. "Then whatever it is… it knows you're awake now."

Sarah nodded.

"And it knows we're coming."

Crossroads of Fire

Safehouse – Late Afternoon

The mood was different this time.

No celebration. No relief.

The trek back from the site had been quiet, each step weighed down by something none of them could quite put into words — the residue of the shadow on the wall, the whisper of Vel'takar, and Sarah's silent retreat into her thoughts.

Now, the safehouse felt smaller.

The windows glowed with late sun, dust drifting lazily in the shafts of light, but no one noticed. Jack stood by the table, arms crossed, the remnants of a field map spread across it. Victor leaned in beside him, pointing out a circled region on the northern edge of a weathered page. Nora sat on the arm of the battered couch, fiddling with the drone controller — still claiming it was damaged, but suspiciously active again.

Sarah stood at the far end of the room, notebook open, her eyes darting between glyph sketches and her father's translated margins. She didn't speak, but the intensity in her gaze made it clear: something was coming together.

Finally, she broke the silence.

"We have to go east."

Jack looked up. "That's a war zone."

"Not officially," Victor added. "But close enough. You'll be walking into three decades of border conflicts, dried-up loyalties, and factions that shoot before they question."

Sarah didn't flinch. "There's a valley beyond the conflict line. It's not on modern maps — my father only references it once. But the glyphs at the last site matched its astronomical coordinates."

She slid the notebook across the table.

Jack stared at the sketch. A crescent-shaped valley bordered by cliffs, with a constellation diagram traced faintly over the terrain. A symbol pulsed faintly in Sarah's notes.

The same one that had appeared during her dream.

Jack's voice was low. "You think this is it?"

"I *know* it," she said.

Victor frowned. "That's not a lot to go on."

"It's all we've ever had," she replied. "Instinct, fragments, visions."

She glanced at Jack. "You told me once to trust my instincts. I'm telling you now — this is it."

Jack hesitated.

Then nodded. "We move at first light."

Victor groaned. "I just patched my shoulder."

"You can sit this one out," Jack offered.

Victor scoffed. "Like hell I will."

Sarah gave him a half-smile, the first in hours. "Good."

Jack gathered the map, folding it with practiced hands. "Then we prep tonight. Ammo checks, load light. We may not get a second chance."

Nora finally spoke. "And if it's another misdirection?"

Jack looked her dead in the eye. "Then we deal with it. Same as always."

But his voice had steel now. They were running out of time — and whether this valley held the third lock or not, something was pulling them forward.

Something that no longer waited in shadows.

It was watching.

And it was ready.

Nora remained seated on the couch long after the others began their tasks. Her eyes didn't move from the blank controller in her lap — fingers tracing its edges, mind far from the circuitry.

No message.

No reprimand.

No contact.

It had been days since the Order had reached out, and she had reported nothing. That was dangerous. But the silence? That was worse.

The moment she'd uttered *Vel'takar*, she'd known.

Just like the slip about the Order back at the dig site — careless. Impulsive. Emotional.

Two mistakes.

Two more than she was allowed.

She let out a long, quiet breath.

What was happening to her?

Once, she'd been precise. Purpose-driven. She'd embedded herself deep into this operation under strict orders and unwavering conviction. Watch Sarah. Report movement. Gain proximity to the Stone.

But now…

Now, she was uncertain.

It wasn't just that the mission had become complicated. It was *them*. Sarah, with her unshakable instinct. Jack, with his frustrating integrity. Harper and Victor — both hardened, capable men who somehow managed to laugh at the worst of it. And then there was the dream — the presence that whispered not commands, but *truths*.

And worst of all…

There was *doubt*.

Not just in the Order. But in herself.

She wasn't sure when it had started. Maybe back at the cave. Maybe when she first saw Jack put himself in front of danger without hesitation. Or maybe when Sarah touched that podium and the stone had responded like it remembered her.

No one had ever looked at Nora like that stone had looked at Sarah.

She clenched her jaw.

"Don't lose focus," she whispered to herself.

But even that command didn't land the way it used to.

Not with silence on the other end.

Not with shadows that no longer seemed as dark… or as certain.

Chapter Eight: The Valley That Waited

Descent into the Forgotten Valley

The valley revealed itself slowly — not through sweeping views or open terrain, but in how the land changed beneath their boots.

What had begun as cracked stone and brush-choked paths gradually shifted into soft earth covered in thick moss, vines curling like fingers through every crevice. Trees arched overhead in unnatural symmetry, limbs twisted toward the same distant point as if called by some unseen current. Even the air felt different — thicker, but easier to breathe. Like something had been filtering it long before they arrived.

Jack paused at the edge of a narrow ledge, scanning the descent below.

"Tell me that doesn't look like it's been landscaped," he muttered.

Victor, crouched beside him, nodded. "But not by us. Or anyone alive."

Behind them, Harper surveyed the tree line with narrowed eyes. "I've been through this region a dozen times. Never saw anything like this. Wasn't even marked on the old military grid."

Nora didn't speak, but her drone buzzed overhead, sweeping the terrain in wide arcs. Her eyes stayed on the readout — too intently. Jack noticed.

Sarah, meanwhile, had gone still.

She stood several paces ahead, one hand resting lightly on a gnarled root that arched from the hillside like a serpent. Her brow furrowed, her breath shallow.

"It's humming," she said quietly.

Jack stepped toward her. "What is?"

She didn't answer at first. Her eyes drifted across the valley — from the dense thickets, to the oddly uniform ridge line, to the worn stone markers jutting like teeth from the ground.

"Everything," she whispered. "This place… it's not hidden by accident. It was buried — wrapped in something. Not just geography. Intention."

Victor shifted his rifle on his back. "Someone wanted to keep people out."

"No," Sarah said, still staring forward. "Someone wanted to keep something *safe*."

They moved in single file, descending through the underbrush where ancient stone stairs had once been carved but were now barely discernible beneath centuries of sediment and growth. Roots cracked the stone in places, but in others, the steps remained perfectly preserved — untouched by weather or time.

"Almost ceremonial," Harper muttered, running his hand along a groove that shimmered faintly in the morning light. "Like a processional path."

"Or a warning," Jack added, eyes sharp.

Sarah didn't respond. Her focus was somewhere deeper — beneath the moss, beneath the soil, beneath herself. Her fingertips tingled with every step.

By the time they reached the floor of the valley, the light had shifted. It filtered through the trees in narrow beams, illuminating flecks of dust that danced like ash.

Jack called a halt at the edge of a shallow stream. Its water was clear but perfectly still. No movement. No sound. Even birdsong had vanished.

Victor crouched beside the stream, scooping up a small vial of water and holding it to the light. "Nothing's moving in it. Not even bacteria."

"That's not possible," Nora said, her voice sharper than intended.

Sarah looked back at her. "It is here."

The group stood in a silence that felt less like pause and more like reverence.

They were inside something now.

Not a valley.

Not a ruin.

But a memory.

And somewhere ahead — past the trees, past the silence — the lock waited.

The Unseen Watcher

They pressed deeper into the valley, the moss thickening beneath their boots like damp velvet. Vines hung low, brushing shoulders and cheeks.

Trees, impossibly tall, formed a canopy that filtered the light into an eerie, perpetual dusk.

Jack walked point, his steps silent, his rifle cradled loosely in his arms — not out of threat, but instinct. Victor stayed close behind, eyes darting like a man who didn't trust the silence. Harper took rear guard, calm but alert, his gait favoring his healing side.

Sarah moved just ahead of the group's center, following no map — only that familiar internal gravity. She no longer questioned it. The pull toward the next lock was growing with every step, whispering not in words but in sensation. Nora, drone cradled and silent, stayed close to Sarah, the tension behind her neutral expression noticeable only to Jack.

It was Victor who said it first.

"We're not alone."

He didn't say it with panic — just certainty.

Everyone froze.

Jack turned slowly, scanning the tree line. Nothing moved. No rustle, no shadow, no change in light.

"You see something?" he asked.

"No," Victor said, lowering to a crouch, "but I feel it. We're being watched."

Harper nodded. "Had the same gut noise since the ridge. Every instinct says eyes on."

"Could be natural," Nora offered, too quickly. "Local wildlife. Movement from the trees."

Sarah glanced toward her. "But no sound."

Nora didn't answer.

Jack took a slow breath, his voice low. "Whatever's watching us isn't making mistakes. That means it's either smarter than your average predator… or it belongs here."

Victor scanned again. "No footprints, no displaced brush. Nothing human."

Sarah's fingers hovered near the box inside her satchel — the celestial instrument that had carried them from lock to lock. It remained inert. No glow. No pulse.

But her skin prickled.

"This valley is cloaked," she whispered. "Not just hidden. Veiled. Like the Sanctuary from the old glyphs."

Harper muttered, "You think we're inside it?"

"No," she said, eyes narrowing. "I think we're near it."

A sudden shift in air pressure rippled through the trees — a sensation more than a sound. Everyone froze.

Nora turned, slowly scanning the canopy. "Drone's not reading anything. No thermals. No signatures."

"Then we assume worst-case," Jack said. "We keep eyes up. Spread the formation. Quiet from here on out."

Victor gave him a quick nod, and Harper silently adjusted his stance, drawing his sidearm as well. Even Nora's hand found her holster — but her eyes drifted back to Sarah again.

There was something different about the way Sarah walked now — no hesitation, no second-guessing. She wasn't following a trail. She *was* the trail.

And someone else knew it.

Something was watching.

Not out of curiosity.

But out of *recognition.*

Symbols in the Stone

The narrow valley widened into a basin, almost imperceptibly. One moment, the trees pressed in close; the next, they gave way to an opening carved directly into the base of the ridgeline — a natural indentation choked with moss and stone, but unmistakably shaped.

Sarah slowed to a stop.

"It's here," she whispered.

She didn't wait for consensus. She stepped forward, brushing past the veiled foliage. Beneath it, a wall revealed itself — tall, wide, jagged with age. It bore no door, no arch, no manmade seams. But at its center, stretching in a half-moon arc, was a collection of ancient glyphs.

They were shallow — so faded they might've been mistaken for fractures — but Sarah felt them rather than saw them. Her fingers hovered over the stone, drawn as if by gravity.

Jack approached from behind. "This the lock?"

She didn't answer at first.

Then: "It's not like the others. No mechanisms. No devices. Just… symbols."

Victor's voice was low. "What do they say?"

Sarah shook her head. "Not exactly words. More… intentions."

She traced one with her fingertip — a spiraling curve that ended in a broken crescent.

"Guardian. Witness. Memory." She murmured, translating not by logic, but instinct. "Silence. Sacrifice."

Harper stepped up beside her, watching carefully. "You sure this is it?"

"No," she admitted. "But I've never felt this drawn before. Not even in the last cave."

Victor crouched, scanning the base of the wall. "Looks like this whole area was once buried. Could've been a landslide. Or something… deliberate."

Jack stepped back, eyeing the surrounding terrain.

"No defenses," he said. "No structural weaknesses. Whatever this was… someone wanted it hidden, not guarded."

"And not opened by accident," Sarah added. Her hand rested now on a center glyph — a complex knot of spirals within spirals. As she touched it, the stone beneath her palm grew warm.

The others stepped back, instinctively.

Then — light.

A faint shimmer crawled across the wall like dew catching sunlight. Glyph after glyph glowed faintly, not illuminating the space, but *confirming it.* A pattern emerged — one that only Sarah seemed to track in real time. Her hand moved from one mark to the next, almost painting in invisible ink.

She wasn't translating.

She was *unlocking*.

"It's not a false lock," she whispered. "But it *knows* I've been to one."

Jack tilted his head. "How?"

Sarah looked up, eyes wide. "The glyphs aren't just symbols. They're… responses. They're *aware*."

A low rumble vibrated through the stone.

Nora flinched. Harper and Victor moved to cover the perimeter, weapons raised.

But nothing attacked. No door opened.

Instead, one glyph in the center pulsed — and faded.

Sarah stared at the spot.

"It's asking for proof."

Jack stepped forward. "Of what?"

"Of me."

The Rite of Silence

The moment the central glyph dimmed, Sarah stepped back — not from fear, but from instinct. The vibration beneath her palm had felt... personal.

Like judgment.

She turned toward the others, her voice quieter than before. "It wants something I haven't given yet."

Nora raised a brow. "You've unlocked two sites already. What more could it possibly need?"

Victor crossed his arms. "Something symbolic? Another puzzle?"

Sarah looked to Jack — not for answers, but for grounding. He gave her a small nod, and for a heartbeat, it was enough.

Then the rumbling returned — brief, deeper this time. Not violent. Not threatening. But resolute.

Sarah turned back to the wall and pressed both palms to the center glyph.

"Do not follow the noise," she whispered, recalling the warning from the cave.

"Silence reveals the true path."

And in that stillness, it came.

A slit in the stone opened — seamless, vertical, impossibly narrow — just wide enough for a single person to enter.

Jack instinctively stepped forward, but Sarah stopped him with a hand on his arm.

"No," she said. "I go alone."

"The hell you do," Jack muttered, bracing.

But she shook her head, eyes steady. "This is the Rite of Silence. It's not about defense or strategy. It's about trust. If you come, it won't open further."

Harper watched the shifting stone and grunted. "Sounds like a trial."

Nora folded her arms. "Or a trap."

Victor simply said, "Then it has to be her."

Sarah gave a small, almost trembling smile. "It's always been me."

She stepped toward the slit. As she did, the opening widened slightly, just enough for her to pass through.

The light changed the moment she entered — not darker, but *denser.* It pressed around her like water. No sound followed. Not her footsteps. Not her breath. Even her heartbeat seemed absorbed by the walls.

The space was narrow but not suffocating. Ahead, the tunnel curved, then opened into a small chamber carved with the same spiraling glyphs. In the center, a pedestal — simple, unadorned — cradled a shallow bowl of black stone.

Sarah stepped forward, reverently.

Inside the bowl: dust. Or maybe ash. Something so fine it moved like smoke when she breathed.

The silence grew heavier.

Then, across the far wall, a glyph flared — brighter than the rest. Sarah moved closer.

The translation didn't come in pieces.

It came all at once.

"Only those who carry memory may protect what remains."

She understood.

This was not just about being called.

It was about being *willing* to remember what others would forget. To bear the weight of the truth — and protect it, even when no one else knew it existed.

She reached out, touched the dust.

The chamber responded.

The glyphs dimmed.

The pedestal retracted.

And the wall behind her began to open — slowly, silently — revealing a hidden passageway leading deeper into the mountain.

Outside, Jack had his ear to the stone when the sound reached him — a breath of wind that hadn't been there before.

He turned sharply.

"She did it," he said.

Victor nodded. "We follow?"

Jack hesitated.

"No," he said. "Not yet."

Because the Rite of Silence wasn't meant to be shared.

Chapter Nine: Embers of the Veil

Arrival in Virelli

An old city layered in stone and secrets — and one too many watching eyes.

The narrow roads into Virelli twisted like veins through hills once thought sacred. They descended into the city just after dawn, dust trailing the armored wheels of their weather-worn vehicle. The transition from the wild to civilization was abrupt — the sudden din of life, of movement, of too many strangers and too many places to hide. Jack hated it.

The city was built upward more than outward. Crumbling staircases wound around buildings stacked like stone organs in a hive, patched with wood and plaster, ancient and new colliding without apology. At its heart stood a towering chapel — smooth-faced stone bleached by centuries of sun, its spire rising above the city like a crooked finger warning the sky.

"This place wasn't on any of the original route maps," Jack muttered from behind the wheel.

"It wasn't considered viable," Victor said from the passenger seat. "Too urban. Too exposed. And yet here we are."

In the back, Sarah stared at the city, one hand on the satchel holding her father's journal, the other gripping the small box recovered from the plateau. "It's here," she said. "It's not a guess."

Flashback – Uneventful Lock Opening

Her voice was steady, but her mind flickered back to the moment in the mountain — after the silence had answered her. After the wall had shifted open.

She had gone in alone. Jack had stayed behind, not by order, but by some instinct that told him he wasn't meant to walk that part of the path.

The passage had been narrow, smooth, and silent as bone. No puzzles. No traps. Just a shallow circular chamber at its end — with nothing in it but a single pedestal bearing the same faint glyph carved into the box from the plateau. She had placed her hand over it.

The stone had recognized her.

The lock had opened.

No sound. No resistance. No fanfare. Just a low, pulsing warmth through her palm — and then a soft light glowing in the rock face behind the pedestal, revealing the next set of glyphs. A direction. Not a location. A bearing that led here — to Virelli.

It had felt too easy.

And somehow… that made her more nervous than the traps.

"Instinct?" Jack asked, glancing at her in the mirror.

Sarah nodded slowly. "But… it's different this time."

Jack caught that.

Different how?

But she didn't elaborate.

Nora looked out the window and frowned. "This is one of the oldest inhabited places in the region. Trade post, then stronghold, then religious site. If Lock Four is hidden under a population center, this is exactly the kind of place it would end up buried."

They parked off a narrow side street. Victor made contact with an old university friend who had relocated to Virelli as a historical site curator. She helped secure lodging in an abandoned archive building near the outer wall — private enough, forgotten enough, with a view that cut clean across the stone skyline.

An hour later, they were standing before the **Chapel of Saint Erren**, said to have been constructed atop ancient ruins. Inside, the air was cool and stale — but laced with some invisible charge.

Sarah stepped in first.

It hit her like a whisper across her chest.

"I've felt this before," she whispered. "But it's… off."

Jack moved in behind her, slow, deliberate. "Off how?"

She shook her head. "Like it's calling me — but not clearly. Like someone else is speaking over it."

Before Jack could press further, footsteps echoed softly from the back of the nave. A figure approached from the shadows beneath the pulpit — tall, robed, with sharp features and eyes too kind to trust at first glance.

"Travelers," he said, voice calm and warm. "You've come seeking the old light, haven't you?"

Jack's hand didn't move from his hip. Nora straightened, just barely.

Sarah took a step forward. "You're the keeper of this place?"

The man bowed slightly. "Caretaker. Guide. I am Father Marcion. And I know why you've come."

Jack's jaw tightened.

Marcion's eyes slid to Sarah, holding too long. "You carry the silence with you."

The words meant nothing. And yet Sarah felt a tremor run up her spine.

He smiled gently. "You are welcome here. But tread carefully. What sleeps beneath Virelli does not always dream alone."

Beneath the City – Unseen Chains

The descent wound downward like a forgotten spiral — too narrow for modern stonecutting tools, too precise to have been shaped by erosion. Cold seeped from the walls. Not the chill of damp stone, but a deeper stillness, as if sound itself avoided these halls.

Their footsteps echoed only once, and then vanished into silence.

Sarah moved ahead, her palm brushing the curved wall for balance. The path dipped again, and lanterns — old, oil-fed things maintained by unseen hands — flickered to life in alcoves carved like shallow graves.

Victor's voice was low. "This wasn't buried. This was *swallowed*."

Harper nodded grimly. "This place has been alive a long time."

They reached the base.

The passage opened into a wide vestibule — domed, circular, and faintly glowing from a central fire bowl that should have gone cold centuries ago. Narrow ventilation shafts ran to the surface, letting in filtered daylight in subtle beams like cathedral light through dust. The floor was perfectly smooth. On the far side stood a high stone door, sealed tight, flanked by two blindfolded attendants draped in charcoal-gray robes.

They didn't speak. Didn't even look up.

Sarah's breath caught. Symbols—crude yet unmistakable—ran the arch of the doorway. She stepped closer. "These glyphs… they're older than anything we've seen before."

"Older than the temple?" Jack asked.

"No," she murmured. "Deeper. Cruder. Like the first attempt to *hold* something in words."

Victor scanned the ceiling. "You realize this place has been maintained. Guarded. Which means… the Order may not even fully understand what they're keeping locked up down here."

Nora, lingering near the rear of the chamber, didn't reply.

But she felt it too. These weren't just ruins. This was **doctrine built over desecration** — the kind of architecture you create when you're not sure if you're honoring something… or making sure it doesn't rise again.

Harper eyed the attendants. "These men. Monastic discipline, maybe? Their hands are scarred from blade training, not ink. Look at the way they stand — perfect angles. Former soldiers, or… zealots."

"They're not the threat," Jack said, stepping past them.

No one tried to stop him.

The sealed door loomed.

Sarah placed her hand against the archway. The stone didn't warm, but it trembled — the faintest shudder, like muscle spasming under old scar tissue.

She drew her hand back. "It *knows* me."

Nora stepped forward. "You've opened other locks. What's different?"

"This one feels…" Sarah hesitated. "Like something went wrong here."

Symbols flared along the doorway — not with light, but with pain. Their shimmer came in pulses, like bruises forming in real time.

Victor frowned. "That's not right."

"No," Sarah whispered. "It's not."

The Silent Mechanism

The door yielded without sound.

Not a scrape, not a grind. Just pressure and surrender — stone shifting against stone like breath held too long.

Beyond it lay a small chamber, circular, maybe twenty feet wide. Unlike the ornate vestibule behind them, this room was barren. No symbols. No altars. Only a single pedestal at the center, plain and dark, carved from obsidian or something older. The walls arced smooth and sterile, curved perfectly into the ceiling like the inside of a sealed lung.

Sarah stepped in first.

The pressure hit her immediately — not physical, but internal. As though something ancient and angry had recognized her before she crossed the threshold.

She reached for the pedestal.

Jack caught her wrist, voice tight. "You sure?"

"No," she whispered. "But I *feel* it."

He let her go.

Sarah pressed her hand flat against the top of the pedestal.

Nothing.

Not at first.

Then… movement.

From deep below, something shifted. A tremor crawled up through the stone, not violent but precise — as if gears had been waiting for her skin to complete their circuit. A faint glyph emerged beneath her palm, glowing dull red, pulsing slowly.

She traced it, and a second line formed. Then a third.

A full symbol: a circle within a square, broken at the edges, like containment shattered.

Sarah's breath hitched.

"It's a warning."

Jack stepped beside her. "Not a map?"

"No. A barrier. Something was meant to be kept *in*. Not *out*."

Victor leaned in. "Then why respond to you?"

"I don't know," she said.

Another glyph bloomed — this one in black, not red, and not glowing. It absorbed the dim light instead of reflecting it. And beneath it, etched shallow and almost missed:

"False light draws true shadow. Guard not the door, but the hollow behind it."

Nora's face paled slightly.

Harper's jaw tightened. "This isn't a lock."

"No," Sarah said. "It's a **mirror.**"

Jack frowned. "Meaning?"

"This is a *test.* It mimics a lock. But there's no path forward from here. Only backward."

Victor's voice dropped. "A false site."

Sarah nodded, slowly.

The air grew colder.

Jack turned toward the door. "Then this is where they wanted us."

"And where we led them," Nora whispered under her breath — too quiet for anyone to hear, but loud enough to echo inside her own skull.

Ashes of the First Flame

Flashback – Circa 1773

The mountain had no name.

It existed on maps only as an elevation reading. No paths. No settlements. Just stone, ice, and centuries of silence. But beneath it… something pulsed. Something waiting.

Callan Virelli arrived before the first snowfall.

Not yet a prophet. Not yet a founder. Just a man out of step with his time — a scholar cast out of the Venetian College of Antiquities for promoting heresies of pre-human symbology and ancient "living languages." He had traveled through Prague, Cairo, even to the foothills of the Caucasus in search of patterns he'd begun to dream long before he ever saw them etched in stone.

He believed there was a deeper history — not of mankind, but of what came *before.*

And then the shard came.

Left in a lead-lined oak box on the steps of his boarding house in the Pyrenees. No sender. No message. Only a symbol burned into the lid — a triangle wrapped around a single black eye, its iris drawn as flame.

The moment he touched it, the visions began.

A voice that didn't echo — it *infested.* A will older than God or empire. Not divine. Not righteous. But full of fire and promise. The voice called itself nothing. But it asked a question:

"Shall I be loosed?"

Virelli had no answer. Only the impulse to follow.

The shard hummed with heat when he passed certain stones. It responded to symbols he hadn't known he could read. It *led.* And it brought him to this mountain — and to the cave within.

The structure was unnatural. Not made, but grown — shaped by purpose. There were no markings on the outside. Only within, carved in looping lines and sacred geometry, were symbols that whispered through his veins like old blood.

At the center stood a podium of smooth basalt, carved in a way no chisel could mimic.

He placed the shard atop it.

The air thickened.

His breath slowed.

The stone beneath his feet thrummed — not a tremor, but a *heartbeat.* The glyphs on the walls shimmered in dull crimson. The podium pulsed once, twice.

And then the voice returned.

You are not the one who opens the gate. But you are the one who finds them.

Build them. Shape them. Lie to them, if you must. But bring them to me.

The Guardian must come willingly.

What Virelli saw next changed him forever.

He saw the *Stone* — luminous, contained, locked behind five sacred doors not of metal, but of meaning. He saw the **Steward**, old and cloaked in light, burdened by memory. He saw the **Sanctari**, blade in hand, watching the door.

And he saw the **Guardian** — never the same, always awakening.

Then he saw *him.*

Vel'takar — not flesh, but force. Fire without smoke. Hunger without mouth. Reaching always.

And always *denied.*

I cannot pass the gates. But I can reach those who will.

Help me find the path. And I will make you eternal.

Callan Virelli wept. Not in fear — but in *awe.*

When he emerged from the mountain, days later, he carried the shard in a sealed iron cylinder and burned his real name behind him. The world would come to know him only as **The First Flame**.

He began recruiting — not soldiers, but **believers**. Thinkers. Outcasts. Those who had seen patterns behind the veil of religion, empire, and superstition. Men and women who could be shaped. Who could wait. Who could *build.*

And so, the **Arcane Order** was born.

First as a circle of whispers in France. Then a monastery. Then cells, scattered across continents, working silently, infiltrating the sciences, the clergy, and the nobility.

Not an army. A society.

Because empires fall.

But *faith endures.*

The Vault of the Flame

Temple Interior — Nightfall

The catacombs beneath the chapel were colder than expected — not just in temperature, but in presence. The air was too still, too old. Dust didn't stir here. It had settled generations ago and never moved again.

Jack moved cautiously, his hand brushing the wall for balance as the passage narrowed. The priest's torch illuminated only a few feet ahead, flickering against carved walls that didn't resemble burial chambers — they resembled design. Intent. Geometry with memory.

Victor followed behind, rifle slung but eyes alert. "This isn't built like the rest of the temple," he muttered. "It's cleaner. Reinforced."

"Vaulted," Harper added from the rear. "Like they wanted this place to outlast everything above it."

Sarah said nothing. She didn't need to. The pull had returned — low and steady, like a river deep beneath her skin. She wasn't afraid. But her breath caught with every step closer to whatever waited at the end of the hall.

The passage ended in a broad, circular chamber, shaped like a keyhole. Its domed ceiling was etched with the same double-ringed sigil they'd seen in the chapel above — the eye within the triangle, flames licking its edges. A single dais rose in the center of the room, and atop it rested a glass vault.

Within that vault lay two things:

A shard of impossibly dark glass — no reflections, no edges. Just a sliver of absence that seemed to devour light.

And beside it, draped in ceremonial robes long faded to gray, the perfectly preserved body of a man.

Victor whispered, "Virelli."

The priest stepped forward and bowed low. "The First Flame. Our founder. His body has not decayed in over two hundred years."

Jack studied the vault. "Why the glass case?"

"To contain the shard," the priest said softly. "It is… not safe. Even now."

Sarah was already scribbling into her journal, her eyes flitting between the glyphs on the surrounding walls and the sigil on the man's robe. "This isn't preservation," she said. "It's worship. They built a reliquary. And they didn't just honor him — they honored what he carried."

"The shard," Harper said.

Nora remained at the edge of the chamber, her arms crossed. She hadn't looked directly at the glass. Her face was tense, jaw tight, as though remembering something she'd never meant to.

"Have you ever opened the vault?" Sarah asked the priest.

He shook his head immediately. "No. None are allowed. It is sealed by rite and by flame. Only when the Guardian returns will the Light judge its truth."

Sarah frowned. "What light?"

Before the priest could answer, the glyphs along the wall shimmered faintly — the same dull crimson that had once greeted Virelli in his vision centuries ago. The shard inside the vault pulsed once.

And Sarah dropped to one knee.

Her hands clutched the floor. Her vision blurred. A soundless pressure poured into her skull — not pain, but clarity. Images. Shapes. Lines forming in her mind like old memories written in stars.

Snow. Rock. A veil of mist. A peak shrouded in ancient ice.

A voice, calm and female, echoed through her spine:

"You are almost there, but you have strayed. Return to the rhythm. The wound must be healed before the path can open."

Jack rushed to her side, steadying her. "Sarah—?"

"I'm fine," she gasped. "It's the next site. I saw it."

She pointed to the far wall — a carving too eroded to identify clearly, but beneath the surface, something felt alive. "That's not a tomb. It's a warning."

Harper helped her up. "What did you see?"

"A mountain," she said breathlessly. "Covered in cloud and frost. But not just hidden… buried in time."

The priest stepped forward again. "The shard speaks to you."

Jack turned sharply. "You knew it was still active?"

The priest faltered. "I… I only suspected. But its warmth never faded. We believed it still served the flame."

Jack's face hardened. "You serve the Order."

That stopped the priest cold. His eyes darted to the vault, then to Sarah. "I serve the truth. As all of us were meant to."

Nora stepped forward slowly. "Your version of the truth burns people."

Sarah straightened. Her heartbeat had steadied, but something in her chest still thrummed like a held note. "This wasn't just a vault. It was a test."

Victor nodded. "And we passed."

Jack turned to the team. "We move at dawn."

As they exited the vault, Sarah glanced one last time at the shard — still pulsing softly, like a slow heartbeat waiting to rise.

Behind her, Harper murmured to Victor, "That wasn't just a lock…"

"No," Victor replied. "That was a wound."

A Sudden Stillness

The wind had died overnight.

It wasn't just quiet — it was *still.* The kind of still that wrapped around the skin and settled in the lungs. No birdsong. No shifting of stone. Even the loose banners of the temple walls hung limp, as though breath itself had paused.

Jack stood near the gate, one boot on a stone step, eyes scanning the horizon. The pack on his back creaked slightly as he shifted weight. Sarah was inside, finishing her notes on the wall carvings. Nora leaned against the temple's side column, flipping through her comm device for the third time in an hour — no signal. Nothing from the Order. Nothing from anyone.

Victor and Harper quietly checked their weapons. Neither had slept more than an hour, but neither complained. They knew what the silence could mean in a place like this.

"Something's wrong," Harper muttered under his breath.

Jack didn't respond. He was thinking the same thing.

Inside the temple, Sarah closed her father's journal and ran a hand across the stone altar one final time. Her vision from the night before still echoed behind her eyes — the mountain wrapped in frost, the hidden place calling her forward. She was ready to move. She felt it in her bones.

But when she stepped into the temple courtyard, something caught in her chest.

Jack was looking at her — not just watching, *looking*. His expression unreadable, but his eyes tracked every step she took like he was counting heartbeats. It wasn't duty. It wasn't suspicion.

It was something deeper.

"Everything ready?" she asked.

He nodded slowly. "Just waiting for the sky to give us permission."

Sarah smirked, but the mood was too tight for levity.

Victor approached with a faint cough. "We move southeast by midday. I'll lead the first stretch. There's a ridgeline not far from here that should hide our approach toward the valley."

Harper added, "Assuming the route hasn't changed."

Jack nodded again but didn't lower his gaze.

Then, from the archway, Nora spoke — her voice sharper than usual.

"Sarah," she said. "Did the dream tell you *how far* this valley is?"

Sarah frowned. "No. Just a sense of direction. A pull."

Nora glanced down at her comm once more, still nothing. Her knuckles whitened as she gripped it.

"I don't like flying blind," she muttered, more to herself than anyone else.

Sarah didn't respond — not directly. Instead, she looked toward the mountains in the east.

"We're not flying blind," she said softly. "We're following something older than maps."

Then the ground trembled.

Just once — a subtle vibration beneath their feet, like the world exhaling.

Jack's hand moved instinctively to his rifle.

Harper turned his head sharply, squinting toward the tree line.

Victor's voice dropped to a whisper. "That wasn't an earthquake."

Jack drew his weapon. "Positions."

No orders needed.

Everyone scattered to cover.

And from the shadows of the lower courtyard, something stirred.

The Priest's Final Move

It started with a voice.

Low. Chanted. Carried not by air, but by resonance — as if it rose from the stone itself.

Then came the figures.

Cloaked in deep crimson and bone-white masks, they emerged from the lower levels of the temple — from passages no one had marked, through doors that had appeared sealed. Twelve in all. Their movements were slow at first, ritualistic. Each one held a curved blade etched with symbols that shimmered faintly in the dawn light.

Sarah froze.

"Those aren't Order agents," she whispered.

"No," Nora replied grimly. "They're something older."

Harper already had his pistol up. "Cultists?"

Victor narrowed his eyes. "No. Priestly faction. I've seen that kind of garb once before — they answer to something the modern Order pretends doesn't exist."

The chanting grew louder. The lead priest — taller than the others, with a jagged scar cutting across his exposed neck — raised both arms high.

"The Guardian stands among us!" he intoned. "The prophecy returns! She must not flee her purpose!"

Jack shifted closer to Sarah, shielding her with a step. "Well, that's subtle."

The priest's eyes locked onto Sarah.

"You do not yet *know*, but the Flame does," he said. "He *hungers* for your arrival. The door may open… but only if you *choose* to cross it."

The moment hung — heavy, breathless.

Then everything shattered.

With a sudden, feral cry, the masked priests surged forward.

Gunfire erupted.

Jack and Harper opened fire from opposite sides of the courtyard. Victor moved to intercept the flanking attackers, his shotgun pulsing thunder in the confined space. Nora fired short, sharp bursts — precise, surgical.

But they weren't trying to win.

They were trying to *take* Sarah.

"Eyes left!" Harper barked. "They're closing—!"

Sarah turned just in time to see a masked priest vault a column and tackle her from the side. They both went down hard — her breath driven from her chest.

The man didn't try to kill her. He only wrapped his arms around her and shouted a single word in the ancient tongue.

"Sacrifica!"

A blinding flash — smoke.

Another figure grabbed Sarah's arm.

She kicked, twisted, but there were too many hands.

Then she was gone — pulled back through one of the lower doors.

"Sarah!" Jack's voice cut the air, raw and livid.

He surged forward — too late.

The hidden door slammed shut behind her.

Then silence returned — broken only by the groans of dying priests and the acrid stench of smoke.

Jack turned toward Victor.

"They're taking her to him."

Victor nodded once. "And they won't wait long."

Fallout and Fury

The chamber was still trembling when the last body hit the stone.

Jack stood amid the smoke and echoes, fists clenched, jaw locked tight. His rifle hung at his side, forgotten.

Sarah was gone.

Victor stepped forward, reloading with the calm precision of a man who'd seen too many battles and lost too many friends. "That wasn't the Order's usual style."

"No," Jack growled. "This wasn't coordinated. It was ritual."

"Spiritual faction," Harper added. He was crouched over one of the fallen attackers, flipping the mask free. Beneath it, the face was young. Too young. Eyes glassy. "You see that kind of devotion, you don't get it with paychecks. You get it with promises."

"Or fear," Victor muttered. "Or both."

Nora was off to the side, crouched behind a shattered pillar, watching the sealed door where Sarah had vanished. Her pistol still trembled slightly in her hand.

Harper didn't miss it.

"You okay?"

She nodded too quickly.

Jack wasn't looking at her. His stare was fixed on the door. On the place where Sarah had disappeared. His breath came shallow — not panic. Rage. The kind that boiled slow and precise.

"She was standing next to me," he muttered.

"She was chosen, Jack," Harper said gently. "You weren't going to stop that pull."

"She didn't *choose* this." His voice cracked slightly, like steel under pressure. "They took her. And I let it happen."

Nora stood. Her voice was quieter. "No. They planned for this. You reacted. You kept the rest of us alive."

Jack didn't reply. He just looked at the blood on the floor and the smoke curling along the ceiling like a silent accusation.

Then he turned to Victor. "How fast can we breach that door?"

Victor gave a tight smile. "Give me five minutes. Maybe less."

Jack nodded once. "She's not staying here. Not for *them*."

He looked at Harper. "You in?"

Harper gave a dry chuckle. "I'm too old to run, but I'm too stubborn to sit this one out."

Nora stepped up beside them. "I'll help."

Jack turned to her slowly.

Her eyes didn't waver.

"I don't care what they say about me," she added quietly. "But I *do* care what she thinks. And I'm not letting them take her."

The three of them stood in the rising light, broken stone, and smoke swirling around them.

Then Jack raised his weapon, eyes hard.

"Let's bring her home."

Captive in the Chamber

Sarah's consciousness returned in fragments.

Cold stone beneath her. The smell of incense and something older—charred wood, or maybe burned blood. A flickering sound, steady and unnatural, like breath caught in a glass throat.

She didn't remember being dragged.

Didn't remember the moment her vision went black—only the priest's face as she was seized. Calm. Purposeful. Like he believed something sacred had just happened.

She tried to sit up, but her wrists were bound with braided cord—slick and tight like ceremonial rope rather than military restraints. Her shoulders ached from being carried, but otherwise she was unharmed.

That was the most disturbing part.

They weren't trying to hurt her.

They were *waiting.*

She looked around.

The chamber was domed, wider than the one before. Smooth basalt again—no sharp corners, no seams. A dais stood in the center, elevated by three shallow steps, and upon it sat a stone basin filled with a thick, black liquid that didn't reflect light. Above the dais, a circular skylight had been carved into the stone ceiling—an aperture perfectly aligned with the rising sun. It would strike the basin in full just before noon.

Carved into the walls were glyphs. Not the ones from her father's journal or the ancient locks. These were more angular. Harder. Familiar, but wrong—like the language of the stone after being twisted through someone else's tongue.

She was not alone.

The priest stood just beyond the basin, dressed now in full ceremonial garb—layers of dark robes etched with gold thread in the same harsh shapes that marked the chamber walls. He held a staff carved from bone and ash, and his eyes glowed faintly—not with madness, but with belief so absolute it burned.

"You are not meant to fear," he said gently. "Only to open."

Sarah said nothing. Her heart pounded, but her face remained still.

"The Guardian must come willingly," he whispered. "And so you did. Not because we forced you. Because the path called you. And now, here, the Flame waits."

Sarah struggled against her bindings. "You don't even know what the Flame *is*."

The priest stepped forward. "It is light in shadow. Fire unbound. Not a god. Not a demon. But the truest answer to the question buried in every soul: *Why must we suffer to find meaning?* The Flame burns that question away."

He raised the staff, and the basin began to ripple—though no wind stirred.

"You have been chosen by ancient right," he continued. "The locks knew you. The glyphs obey you. And the stone waits for you. But you are still unformed."

"I'm not giving you anything," Sarah said.

"I'm not asking you to." His voice remained soft. "I'm asking you to *see*."

He gestured toward the basin.

A shape began to emerge from the black liquid—not a creature, but a reflection.

Her reflection.

But not quite.

This version of Sarah had no shadow. Her eyes were all white. Her lips moved soundlessly.

The priest lowered his head. "You are the door. We are simply the key."

Sarah's pulse surged.

Then—suddenly—she felt it.

Not just the pull. The *push.*

Something inside her chest flared, like instinct wrapped in heat. Not anger. Not fear.

Rejection.

The chamber was wrong. The glyphs were wrong. This entire place *reeked* of counterfeit design—a shadow play meant to mimic the sacred truth of the locks.

This wasn't part of the path.

This was *inversion.*

"I don't belong here," she said aloud.

The reflection twisted.

"You were born here," the priest answered.

But Sarah smiled—something defiant, something ancient.

"No," she said, voice rising with certainty. "I was *called.* And this isn't where the call leads."

The basin roared as the reflection shattered.

The priest reeled back in horror.

And behind them—barely audible—stone began to grind.

The rescue had begun.

Flames and Reckoning

The chamber doors exploded inward.

Not from an explosive charge—but from Harper's shoulder, driving forward with the weight of a man who refused to die twice. He staggered, caught his footing, and raised his sidearm in one clean motion.

"Step away from her," he growled.

Jack was right behind him, blade drawn instead of a rifle—moving fast and precise, his eyes already tracking every shadow. Victor swept in low, taking the flanks. His rifle barked once, and a cloaked zealot dropped near the altar steps.

The priest turned, his shock not from fear—but betrayal. "You would *profane* the Rite?"

"I'd rather profane it," Jack said, "than let you rewrite it."

The guards scattered, realizing too late they were outnumbered and outmatched.

Sarah sat at the center of it all, ropes burned away by her own hand—though she wasn't sure *how*. The bindings had turned to ash when her heart flared with refusal. Her fingertips still trembled, not from fear, but from power she hadn't intended to call.

The basin shattered behind her as a stray round struck the dais. Black liquid spilled over the steps like blood. The priest screamed—not in pain, but in despair.

"You've ruined everything!" he howled. "The Flame was ready!"

"The Flame," Victor muttered, leveling his weapon, "can go to hell."

Harper moved to Sarah, one hand steadying her. "You alright?"

She nodded, slowly. "He wanted me to come willingly."

"You didn't."

"No," she said. "I *chose.*"

Jack helped her stand. Their eyes met—just for a beat. Whatever else had been whispered in that chamber, whatever vision the basin had offered, it hadn't taken hold.

The priest dropped to his knees, weeping.

"You don't understand. I've waited all my life. I built this sanctuary for him. He *needs* her."

Jack stepped forward. "So you can offer her up like a sacrifice?"

The priest looked up—tear-streaked and smiling. "No. So he can *step through* her."

The room fell into silence.

Victor knelt beside the priest and yanked a chain from beneath his robes. Attached was a jagged piece of dark glass, caged in silver and shaped like a distorted shard of obsidian. It pulsed once, then went still.

"The shard," Victor murmured. "The one from the Order's founding."

Sarah's eyes narrowed. "That's how he heard it."

Victor nodded grimly. "It's not just a relic. It's a conduit."

Harper tilted his head. "A speaker."

Jack straightened. "Or a *beacon*."

The priest laughed softly. "It calls to him. It always has. And when she touched the basin—it answered."

Victor pocketed the shard, then jabbed a tranquilizer into the priest's neck. "Time to sleep, prophet."

The old man collapsed.

Sarah leaned on Jack, breathing hard.

And then—suddenly—her knees gave way.

She hit the ground, gasping as light filled her vision. Not from the room. From within. A rush of heat and clarity. Symbols racing behind her eyelids. Cold wind and blinding snow.

A mountain peak. Wrapped in mist. Hidden behind a veil of cloud and frost.

The *real* lock. Her voice was barely audible, but her eyes told the rest. Not fear. Not confusion. *Conviction.*

She looked to Jack, then Harper, her gaze steady. "It's the same place I saw before — the mountain, the veil of frost. I didn't just imagine it. It called again. Stronger this time. Like it knows I'm ready."

Victor's brows furrowed. "The buried site from earlier?"

She nodded. "It's not just the next lock. It's been waiting for me. All this time."

Jack was already catching her, guiding her gently down. "Sarah—what is it?"

Harper and Victor rushed over.

Sarah's voice trembled, but it held a calm certainty beneath the strain.

"We have to go north."

Victor looked to Harper. "A vision?"

Harper nodded. "Looks like."

Sarah opened her eyes, still dazed.

"It's not just a lock," she said. "It's a wound. We were never supposed to come here."

She looked at the shattered basin. At the broken priest.

"This place… was a scar."

Harper helped her up. "Then let's stop bleeding."

Chapter Ten: The Frozen Veil

The Long Climb

Snow crunched underfoot — dry, brittle, the kind that screamed against silence.

The frozen range loomed above them, a jagged procession of white-tipped teeth disappearing into the gray morning sky. Visibility came in bursts — wind stripping clouds away only to replace them with fog a breath later.

Victor moved with practiced ease, his steps measured despite the incline. Jack followed a few paces back, head down, rifle slung across his chest. He checked the trail behind them frequently, eyes sharp even when the rest of him seemed calm.

Sarah was quiet. Not winded, not slowing, but... somewhere else. Her gloved hand stayed near the pouch that held the star map and her father's journal, as though their weight anchored her.

Jack noticed.

"You good?" he asked, voice low.

She nodded, not meeting his eyes. "Just… listening."

"To what?"

She hesitated. "Everything. Nothing. It's like the mountain's humming. Or maybe it's me."

Nora, hiking farther back, glanced up at that. Her expression unreadable beneath her scarf.

The trail narrowed. Ice slicked the rocks, and every step became a negotiation. Harper, bringing up the rear, grunted as he caught his balance. "Next time we chase a mythical lock, maybe somewhere tropical."

Jack didn't laugh. But his mouth twitched.

Victor signaled a stop near a bend that overlooked a distant crevasse. He crouched, studying the terrain ahead. "We'll have to scale the eastern ridge. The lower passes are snowed in."

Sarah joined him. "The vision — the path was buried. Like it wanted to stay hidden."

Jack scanned the skyline. "So how do we find what doesn't want to be found?"

Sarah didn't answer. Instead, she pointed toward a cluster of rocks partially swallowed by frost. A symbol — faint but familiar — had been etched into their surface.

The triangle. The eye. But older. Rougher. Like it had been carved by a trembling hand centuries ago.

Victor frowned. "That's not new."

"No," Sarah murmured. "Someone was here before us."

Harper stepped closer, voice dry. "And judging by the lack of return path, they didn't leave the way they came."

Nora's gaze lingered on the symbol. Then on Sarah. "This is it, then?"

Sarah nodded slowly. "We're close."

The wind shifted.

Somewhere above them, snow dislodged from the cliffs — a distant, muffled roar echoing through the mountains like a warning.

Jack didn't flinch.

But he stepped closer to Sarah.

Just in case.

Echoes Beneath the Ice

They found the first corpse beneath a veil of ice.

Victor brushed the snow aside with a gloved hand, revealing a weather-worn satchel frozen to the stiffened remains of a man curled inward, as though he'd died trying to keep something out — or in.

Jack crouched beside him, eyes narrowing. "No animal sign. No trauma."

"Just stopped," Victor said. "Like his heart gave up."

Sarah stayed back, breath caught in her throat. The body was old — decades at least — but the coat bore a faint symbol she recognized. Not modern. Crude. Stamped onto leather like a brand.

The triangle again.

The eye.

The flame.

"The Order's been here," she whispered.

Nora looked up sharply. "Before it was even called that."

Victor turned toward her. "You know something?"

Nora's expression was carefully blank. "Only rumors. Failed expeditions. Lost seekers."

Sarah moved slowly now, pulled forward by something more than curiosity. Around a bend in the trail, partially buried beneath centuries of frost, was a wall.

Stone.

Man-carved.

And unmistakably *wrong*.

It didn't belong to the surrounding geology. The shape, the angles — too smooth, too symmetrical. A forgotten structure built into the mountain, sealed by time and snow.

The team stood in silence.

Jack brushed frost from a groove in the stone — revealing an inscription just beneath the surface.

Sarah's eyes widened. "That's the same script I found in the cave… just older."

She stepped forward, notebook in hand, copying the symbols as they appeared. Her pencil shook slightly in the wind.

Then her voice dropped. "This isn't a temple."

Jack looked over. "What is it?"

She didn't respond right away.

Then: "A tomb."

Harper's voice was low. "For what?"

Sarah looked up. Her breath clouded in the frigid air, but she felt no cold.

"Not *what. Who.*"

Victor circled the edge of the stonework, fingers tapping lightly along the seams. "This place was sealed. Not forgotten — intentionally buried."

"And whoever came before us tried to break it open," Jack added, motioning to the frozen remains scattered along the higher ledge.

The wind howled through the pass again — louder this time, like something laughing behind the mountain's bones.

Harper knelt beside the body — not in reverence, but routine. The habit of a man who had once cataloged every piece of evidence like it might be the key to closing a case that would haunt him otherwise.

The coat was thick, stitched from heavy wool and leather long outdated, but functional. As he unfastened the outer pocket, frost cracked across the seams. Inside, tucked against the stiff chest, was a small leather-bound book.

"A journal," Harper said, lifting it free. The cover was cracked with age, warped from moisture, but the latch still held.

He stood slowly and handed it to Sarah. "Found it on the first body. Judging by the others up there—" he nodded toward the frozen ledge, "this guy wasn't alone."

Sarah opened the latch and gently peeled the first few pages apart. The ink had bled in places, but most of the entries were intact. Dated — 1910, 1911… all written in precise, flowing script. The first few pages were routine — weather conditions, elevation markers, references to topography.

Then the tone shifted.

She read aloud:

"The benefactors insist we are close. They call themselves seekers of illumination. Men cloaked in ritual and riddles, funding expeditions under the guise of historical pursuit. But their symbols — the eye, the flame, the whispers in their sleep — none of this is academic. They fear something here, as much as they desire it."

"They believe the mountain guards a relic from before time. They speak of a stone that reveals truth and unbinds fate. I thought it madness… until the frost began to hum beneath our boots."

Sarah swallowed hard.

"There's more."

She turned another page. The handwriting had grown erratic.

"Last night, the snow turned black in my dream. Not from storm — but smoke. Something *watched* from within the stone. One of the initiates — young, proud, unafraid — he touched the outer glyphs. He hasn't spoken since. Just weeps. Screams when we come near."

"The priests — they don't pray. They *offer*. And whatever listens… it does not love them."

Nora looked sharply at the entry. "This was early Order," she said. "Before the structure. Before the corporate arm."

Jack's voice was low. "Before they had rules."

Sarah flipped to the last legible page.

"We cannot proceed. The door will not open. Not for us. It's not locked in the traditional sense — it resists us. Like the mountain itself is *judging*."

"If you find this — turn back. The stone does not want us. And what does want us is worse."

She closed the journal slowly, as if sealing something in.

"I think the mountain protected itself," she said quietly. "Or maybe Vel'takar did. Either way, they weren't worthy."

Victor stepped back from the stone face, eyeing the symbols with fresh wariness.

"So what makes us different?"

Sarah looked down at the journal, then to the bodies above.

"Because I wasn't *sent* here," she said. "I was *called*."

The Door Beneath

Exterior – Mountain Pass, Late Afternoon

The wind shrieked through the upper pass, rattling ice across the rocks like a warning too old to understand.

Sarah traced the last line of text from the frozen journal, her glove moving slowly over the brittle ink.

"Those who break the silence awaken flame."

She stepped back, breath shallow. "That phrase… it was in my dream."

No one answered at first.

Then Jack, low and even: "Then we tread lightly. Or not at all."

The wind howled again — louder this time. Not a gust, but a *voice*. Mocking. Laughing behind the mountain's bones.

They moved as one.

Up toward the carved ridge where the journal had led them, toward a fractured seam in the rock wall partially hidden behind a drift of snow. As Sarah approached, her fingertips tingled — not from cold, but recognition. This was no cave.

It was a *threshold.*

She turned back. "This is it."

Jack gave a nod. "Let's move."

They passed into the mountain.

Interior – Mountain Cavern

The path narrowed to a tunnel just wide enough for single-file movement. The walls were strangely smooth, unnaturally curved — like shaped glass instead of stone. No tools had carved this. No time had weathered it.

Only *intention* had touched these walls.

Sarah walked near the front, her eyes flicking between the faint etchings barely visible in the stone and the growing pressure behind her sternum — the same pressure she'd felt in the dream.

They descended for minutes that felt like hours, each step pulling them deeper into silence.

Then the tunnel widened.

They entered a low cavern, and the air changed again — denser, warmer, as though the earth were exhaling something old.

No one spoke.

Sarah turned slowly in place — then stopped.

There it was.

The far wall was blank, smooth, unbroken — except for a circular indentation in its center. Around it: spiraled carvings, half-fused into the stone. And in the middle of the spiral, a familiar shallow basin.

Her voice came out barely above a whisper. "This is the door."

Jack joined her side, eyes sharp. "Doesn't look like it opens easily."

"Not to hands," she said. "But maybe…"

She pulled the box from her pack and removed the device — the celestial mechanism from the plateau, the one with the warm stone core. As she stepped forward, it responded — faint light bloomed inside its heart.

The spiral shimmered.

Sarah raised the stone.

A pulse — low and steady — vibrated the chamber.

And something behind the door *stirred.*

She pressed the stone into the center basin.

The spiral rotated.

Glyphs appeared — not luminous, but **burned** into the surface, as though seared by an invisible fire.

Nora murmured, "What language is that?"

"Not a language," Victor muttered. "That's a *mark.*"

Sarah's eyes were wide. "It's his."

"Vel'takar," Jack said flatly.

The air turned colder.

As Sarah translated the marks, her breathing hitched. "It's more than a door. It's a seal. A warning. And a threshold."

The device in her hand began to dim.

She flinched — pulling her hand back.

The spiral recessed. The door did not swing open.

It *sank* — layer by layer, dissolving downward into the rock like ash falling in reverse.

Beyond it: **darkness**.

But it was not still.

It *breathed.*

Jack stepped forward, eyes hard. "Sarah?"

She didn't speak. She *felt.*

Then, softly, as if through the chamber itself — **a whisper**.

"Shall I be loosed?"

Sarah stiffened.

Harper moved behind her, muttering, "That's not a metaphor, is it."

Victor raised his rifle, keeping the barrel low but steady. "We're being invited in. Question is, by who."

Jack took one more step — and felt the hairs rise on his arms.

Sarah whispered, "This is the place from my vision. This is the real lock."

Behind her, the stone in her hand went cold.

Into the Breach

Interior — Fourth Lock Chamber, Evening

The air changed the moment they crossed the threshold.

Not colder. Not warmer. Just… still. As if the mountain itself was holding its breath.

Sarah moved slowly, her boots silent on the stone. The chamber ahead widened into a vaulted, circular cavern. Unlike the others, this place had no inscriptions, no iconography. Just curved walls, unnaturally smooth, and a single door embedded at the far end — thick, seamless, and ancient.

But it wasn't the door that stopped her. It was the space before it.

Jack stepped to her side, eyes narrowed. His hand hovered near his sidearm.

"There's something wrong with the air," he muttered. "Feels like it's pressing in."

"It's not air pressure," Harper said quietly, running a hand along the stone. "It's dead silence. Even caves echo. This one's absorbing sound."

Nora adjusted her sensor. "EM field just spiked. No cause. No source."

Victor said nothing. He was already turning in a slow circle, watching the walls.

Sarah stepped toward the door — just one step.

Her stone flared to life in her pack, warmth pulsing against her lower back like a warning. She froze.

"Something's here," she said.

Jack was already watching her. "What kind of something?"

"I don't know. But this… this isn't like before."

The stone glowed faintly, but it wasn't calling her forward. It was holding her back.

She moved toward the wall opposite the door, her steps drawn more by dread than instinct. As her gloved hand brushed the surface, dust fell away from an indented shape — tall, human-shaped… as if something had once stood embedded in the wall, or had tried to come through it.

Nora stepped forward to shine her light — but the beam bent oddly at the edge of the indentation, warping like it was skimming oil on water.

Sarah touched the center.

Nothing.

Then—

The glyphs began to emerge.

Not carved. Not etched.

They *bled* into the stone like ink into cloth — jagged, wrong, and in no pattern she recognized. Not the Stone's language. Not her father's records. Something older. Or darker.

The stone in her pack went cold.

She stepped back fast.

"Don't touch anything," she said quickly. "It's not ours."

Harper raised an eyebrow. "Ours?"

She didn't answer. Her eyes were fixed on a single symbol glowing near the indentation — a spiral of ash-gray, with a core that pulsed red like an open wound.

Jack moved to her side again. "You know what that is?"

"No," she said. Then, quieter: "But it wants me to."

Victor crouched near the far door, scanning it with his handheld device. "Still sealed. No obvious trigger. But someone — or something — has tried to breach it. Multiple times."

Sarah nodded absently. "Vel'takar."

That stopped them all.

"You think it's… here?" Harper asked.

"No. Not yet." She stared at the door. "But it's been here. Or tried to be. This isn't just a lock. It's a barrier."

Nora's voice was tight. "And we just walked into the same space as whatever's been pushing on it for centuries?"

Sarah moved back to the center of the room and took out the stone. Its surface was dull. Lifeless.

"It's testing me," she said. "This place. The lock. Or maybe the thing behind it. To see if I'll open it without thinking."

Jack's eyes narrowed. "Then we don't. We regroup. Rethink."

Sarah shook her head slowly. "We do. But not now. Not like this."

She returned the stone to her pack and turned to the others.

"We set camp just outside. We rest. We wait. And I… I try to listen."

Harper gave her a look. "To what? Rocks?"

"No," she said.

"To the part of me that hasn't lied to us yet."

The chamber stayed silent.

But as they left, the spiral on the wall pulsed once — slow, red, and patient.

The Trial of the Fourth Lock

Interior – Fourth Lock Chamber (Return), Nightfall

They returned just before night swallowed the peaks.

The wind had quieted, the clouds pressed low against the jagged ridges above. The light within the chamber had changed — no longer the strange flatness of earlier. Now, a glow seeped from the seam around the great stone door.

Sarah walked in first.

The others followed close but slow, their eyes drawn toward the spiral still pulsing on the far wall — red, steady, wrong.

"I think it knows we're back," Harper muttered, not looking directly at it.

"No," Sarah said quietly. "It's *waiting*."

She approached the podium that had risen during the night — a thing none of them had seen appear. It hadn't been there before. Now it stood like it had always existed: smooth, flawless stone with no tool marks and no decoration, save a hollow at its center.

Sarah pulled the stone from her pack. Its surface was no longer cold — it shimmered like liquid moonlight.

Jack stepped beside her. "You sure about this?"

She nodded. "No. But I have to be."

He watched her. Something in his chest tugged sharply — not fear, not duty. Something closer to a plea.

But he didn't stop her.

Sarah placed the stone into the hollow.

Nothing happened.

Then the room went dark.

No gradual dimming. No flicker.

Just absolute black.

Jack swore. "Sarah—?"

"Quiet," she said.

A faint vibration hummed under their feet.

Then the glyphs lit up across the far wall — the *true* ones this time. Not the bleeding spiral, but the clean, flowing script of the Guardian's language. Sarah stepped forward instinctively, translating before the words had even fully formed.

Trial is not strength.
Trial is not sacrifice.
Trial is sight.
See what was hidden.
Know what must be denied.
Only the unseen may open the gate.

"I've seen this before," Sarah whispered. "The false door… it wasn't just a warning. It was a veil."

She turned to the stone door. The glow had retreated. Now it was dull again — closed, inert.

Victor looked to Jack. "What's she seeing we're not?"

"I don't know," Jack muttered. But he didn't look away from her.

Sarah pressed a hand to the door.

The glyphs behind her flared in response.

Her eyes fluttered shut.

And then — silence.

But only for the others.

Inside Sarah's mind, light bloomed.

She saw five shapes — standing in an arc: The Steward. The Sanctari. The Guardian. And two others she couldn't name. Behind them: a massive doorway of nothingness. Darkness wrapped in flame. And behind that — the Stone.

But something else moved in the vision.

A shape of smoke and ash.

Watching her.

Testing.

She reached forward.

A voice — not hers — echoed:

"Not all doors must open. Not all truths must be known. But if you are Guardian... you must choose."

Her hand touched the flame in the vision.

Back in the chamber — the door split open with a low grinding sigh.

A passage waited beyond.

Still. Silent. Untouched.

Sarah staggered.

Jack caught her.

"I saw it," she said. "Not the Stone. Not yet. But the edge of it."

She looked into his eyes.

"This was the Fourth Lock."

Chapter Eleven: The Reckoning Below

Beneath the Seal

The mountain held its breath.

A silence fell over the snow-drenched plateau, deep and immediate, like the world itself was waiting. The final lock—its form hidden in ice and myth for generations—had just opened, and with it, a chill deeper than the cold whispered through the team's bones.

Sarah knelt in the snow, hand pressed to the stone platform that had reacted only to her touch. Her breathing was shallow but steady, her eyes focused on something just beyond the edge of thought.

Jack hovered beside her, one hand at her back, the other gripping his rifle. Not as a threat, but as a tether. His voice was low, urgent. "Sarah. You with me?"

She nodded slowly. "It's real. This is it. This is where we were meant to come."

Victor crouched near the edge of the revealed descent, examining the narrow stone stairs that spiraled into blackness. He glanced up. "There's something alive down there."

"More like something waiting," Harper said quietly, scanning the perimeter behind them. "This doesn't feel like an ending. Feels like a damn coiled spring."

Nora hadn't spoken. She stood apart from the group, half-shrouded in shadow, her eyes locked on Sarah. If she felt relief, or dread, or anything in between, it didn't show. But she noticed the change in Sarah — the way the mountain itself seemed to lean toward her now. As if listening.

Sarah pushed herself upright.

"I saw it," she said. "Not just the lock. The way forward. It's down there."

Jack studied her face. She was pale, but not broken. If anything, she looked steadier than he'd seen her since they met. "You sure you can walk?"

"I'm not made of glass, Jack," she said with a tired smile.

"Didn't say you were. I'm just not in the habit of letting people I… trust go marching into unknown pits without asking."

She looked at him.

The moment hung—brief, charged—but she let it pass. "We don't have time. The seal's active. We go now or risk losing the trail."

Victor exhaled sharply. "Then we go carefully. And fast."

Harper stepped beside Jack, his expression unreadable. "We've all seen what happens when we're late."

Jack nodded. "Gear up. Lights on. Tight formation."

He glanced back one last time — at the open horizon, the wind-blown trail that had carried them across deserts, crypts, and betrayal. Then he turned and faced the dark.

Sarah was already descending.

And the seal above them slowly dimmed, as if it had passed its final judgment.

Descent Into Truth

Interior – Below the Mountain Seal, Early Morning

The staircase wound deeper than any of them expected.

Rough-hewn at first, the steps soon became smoother — not worn, but carved with precision, as if made by hands that no longer walked the world. The air thickened with each descent, not with dust, but with presence. Like the mountain wasn't hollow, but dreaming.

Sarah led the way, her lantern casting a soft halo on the walls. Symbols lined them — not in rows, but spirals. Patterns that seemed to move when not directly observed.

"These aren't like the last sites," she murmured, running her fingers just above the stone. "They're older. More… primal."

Victor gave a short grunt. "I'm seeing star paths again. Not navigational. Ritualistic."

"I know," Sarah replied. "They're not meant to guide the body. They guide the awakening."

Jack, close behind her, swept his light across the passage. "Define awakening."

Sarah didn't answer.

Harper brought up the rear, checking their six. He muttered just loud enough for Jack to hear, "She knows where she's going. Even if she doesn't know how."

After nearly half an hour, the path flattened — widening into a chamber unlike any they'd yet encountered. It wasn't massive, but it was flawless. The walls, the floor, even the arched ceiling shimmered faintly with embedded crystalline veins — like stars trapped in stone.

At the far end stood a new structure.

A **mirror**, nearly eight feet tall, encased in obsidian and ringed by a crescent arch of the same pulsating stone as the previous locks.

But this… this one wasn't locked.

It waited.

Sarah approached slowly, her steps almost reverent. The mirror didn't reflect them — not properly. Instead, its surface rippled like liquid shadow, and at its center, something pulsed — a heartbeat not her own.

Victor adjusted his rifle strap. "Is that—?"

"A veil," Sarah breathed. "It's not a door. It's a threshold."

"To what?" Nora asked, her voice low.

Sarah turned. "To where the Stone has been waiting."

No one spoke.

Harper exhaled through his nose. "So we found it."

"No," Sarah said quietly. "We're about to *earn* it."

Jack stepped beside her. "You're sure this is it?"

"I'm sure this is where it begins to *end*."

She lifted her hand toward the arch.

And the mirror pulsed again — stronger this time. The stone at its base glowed faintly with a single glyph: ᛞ — the ancient symbol for passage, or death.

Victor read it aloud. "Only those who carry light will pass."

The room dimmed.

The mirror stirred.

And something on the other side… blinked.

The Guardian's Crossing

Threshold Chamber — Moments Later

No one moved at first.

The mirrored surface rippled again — this time slower, like breath through liquid. A hush fell across the chamber, as though even the mountain were holding its breath.

Sarah lowered her hand.

"I think only one of us can go through," she said softly, without turning around.

Jack stepped closer. "You mean only *you.*"

She nodded. "It's the same feeling I had at the first lock. This is like… the last test. Not a riddle. A reckoning."

Nora frowned. "You're not going in there alone."

"I have to."

Victor eyed the glyph again. "Only those who carry light will pass… Sounds more symbolic than physical."

Harper snorted. "Yeah, and so did the last two traps that almost killed us."

Jack's jaw clenched. "We go together. If it closes behind her, we force it open."

Sarah turned to face him, her eyes steady. "Jack—"

"No," he said. "Don't give me the speech. You're not walking into the unknown alone while I stand around with a rifle and regrets."

She smiled — tired, but touched. "It's not about protection anymore."

He stepped closer, voice low. "It never was."

Her hand found his. Briefly. Warm. Grounding.

Then she looked to the others.

"If anything happens, don't follow. This isn't about bravery. It's about being called."

Victor gave a tight nod. "We'll keep watch. You focus on what's ahead."

Sarah turned back to the veil.

The mirror no longer showed light or shadow — it had become still, expectant. Her steps echoed in the crystalline chamber as she approached it, heartbeat steady, breath deep.

One step. Two.

She placed her palm on the surface.

The veil accepted her.

It shimmered, thinned, then *folded*, like parting fabric.

The swirling veil pulsed like a curtain of mist and starlight, refracting time, and distance. Sarah's form was visible — barely — a wavering silhouette suspended beyond reach. They couldn't call to her. Couldn't cross the threshold.

Jack stared, muscles tense. The urge to follow flared in his chest, primal and automatic. But even a step forward met resistance — not physical, but something deeper, woven into the very air.

"She's still there," Harper murmured. "But not with us."

On the Other Side

(Brief Glimpse — From Sarah's POV)

There was no heat. No cold. Just… silence.

Then — sound. Distant. Rhythmic. Like chanting carried by water.

The space was not a room. It wasn't a hall.

It was memory. Made manifest.

Glyphs shimmered across unseen walls. Symbols moved as if breathing. And at the far end, just beyond a second veil of silver fire, stood a shape — tall, robed, cloaked in luminous stillness.

The *Steward.*

He turned, slowly.

And spoke without lips:

"You have come."

Sarah's lips parted, but no sound left her.

The Steward raised one hand, and behind him… the Stone pulsed. Not yet revealed. But near.

She didn't move.

Not yet.

The real trial had just begun.

The Steward's Testament

Beyond the Veil – Timeless Interior Chamber

Sarah stepped forward slowly.

The chamber didn't feel like a place — not entirely. It felt *held.* Preserved in something older than stone. Light bled from nowhere and everywhere at once, soft, and golden, washing over carved walls etched with swirling glyphs that shifted as she passed. The silence wasn't empty. It was full — with memory, with meaning.

The figure at the far end — the *Steward* — turned fully to face her.

He looked human, and yet not quite. His robes bore the same pattern she'd seen at the observatory and etched in the first lock. His eyes were deep-set, colorless, unreadable. Not ageless — but unyielding. Like time had asked him to move and he had simply refused.

"Sarah Collins," he said, though his mouth did not move. "Daughter of guardians long dormant. Bearer of instinct. Interpreter of memory."

She swallowed hard. "You know my name?"

"I have always known it. As I knew your father's. And his before him. You are the first in three generations to come when called."

She stepped closer, cautiously. "What is this place?"

"A bridge," he said. "Between what was protected… and what must now be decided."

Behind him, light pulsed faintly. The glow formed a half-seen outline — angular, crystalline. Contained.

The *Stone.*

Sarah exhaled sharply.

"It's here."

He nodded once. "Still sealed. Still waiting."

She hesitated. "Then… why call me now?"

"Because the barriers weaken. The Order reaches. The Flame stirs."

"Vel'takar."

The name tasted like ash.

The Steward's voice deepened, resonating through the air. "Born of first betrayal. A corruption formed when the Stone was once used to *command* rather than *heal.* He cannot touch the Stone directly… but he whispers through those who crave it."

Sarah's thoughts spun.

"The Arcane Order," she said. "They think he's divine."

"They see the flame and worship fire. They mistake heat for light."

Her mind flashed to the temple. The priests. The vault. The *shard.*

She looked at the Steward. "Why didn't you stop them?"

"I am the memory. I do not walk the world."

"Then what *am* I?"

He stepped closer. "You are the bridge. Where I cannot act — you can. Where I remember — you choose."

Sarah blinked. "But I don't understand it all yet. I don't know how to fight him. Or how to *use* the Stone—"

"You are not meant to use it," the Steward said, voice suddenly firm. "You are meant to *guard* it."

She froze.

A long silence passed between them.

Then Sarah asked, quietly, "Why me?"

The Steward lifted one hand. The glyphs in the chamber flared. They twisted, interlocked — forming a spiral of scenes, each one a memory. A guardian at a gate. A sanctari falling with sword in hand. A Steward vanishing into shadow. Generations of watchers, fighters, keepers.

"You are the next breath," he said. "Not because of power. But because you listen."

The light behind him dimmed slightly — revealing the Stone more clearly now.

It sat within a suspended crystal shell, not floating but *anchored*, like a heart held in place.

Sarah took one step toward it.

"I don't know if I'm ready."

"Then wait," the Steward said.

"But what if they reach it first?"

"Then they reach nothing," he said. "For without the Guardian… the Stone will never awaken."

She turned to him. "Then what happens now?"

The Steward's gaze softened, just slightly. "Now, you return."

He stepped aside.

The path behind Sarah shimmered open once more — the silver fire beckoning her back.

"And when the final lock calls," the Steward said, "I will come to you. Not here. But where the world burns brighter than shadow."

Sarah looked back once more at the Stone. Then she turned, stepped through the veil—

And the light vanished behind her.

Echoes of the Mark

Interior — Chamber of Still Light, After the Entity's Departure

Silence held them longer than any voice could.

The radiance had vanished, but the walls still hummed with something deeper than light — a silence so full it pressed against their chests. Sarah stood, breath caught somewhere between revelation and weight. Jack didn't touch her, but the tension in his stance had softened, like something had just shifted between them.

Victor leaned against the stone archway, eyes scanning the now-quiet chamber. "I've never seen anything like that," he said. "That wasn't faith. That was… presence."

Harper didn't answer.

He was staring at the floor where the entity had stood — the fading residue of something not meant for the world of flesh and breath. His brow furrowed, like a puzzle was starting to resolve itself across memories he didn't know he still carried.

Sarah turned slowly, her voice steadier than she felt. "That was the Steward."

Jack looked at her sharply. "You're sure?"

She nodded. "It wasn't the first time I've felt it. I saw him once before — not clearly. But I felt it. His light, his calm. He doesn't speak like we do. He offers… truth. But only what we're ready for."

Harper finally broke his silence.

"He left something."

The others looked at him.

"In the hospital," Harper continued, voice low, almost embarrassed. "After I woke up. I thought it was a hallucination — meds or concussion. There was a stone on the bedside table. Black. Smooth. Looked like glass, but it wasn't. I touched it and…"

He stopped, frowning hard.

"…and it was gone. Vanished. Didn't fall, didn't roll off. Just… wasn't there anymore."

Victor raised a brow. "You didn't think to mention that before now?"

"I didn't think it mattered," Harper said. "Hell, I didn't think it was real."

Sarah stepped forward. "It was real. That was a manifestation — a mark. He came to you."

Harper looked down at his hand like he expected something to still be there.

Sarah's gaze flicked between him and Jack, thoughtful now. "He's guiding more than me."

Jack caught her glance, then narrowed his eyes. "What do you mean?"

But Sarah didn't answer — not directly.

She just turned back to the now-dark chamber and said softly, "The stone isn't meant to be found by one. The Guardian opens the way. But others… they stand beside her."

Jack didn't speak. But something in his jaw clenched — not in defiance, but recognition.

Harper said nothing either.

But for the first time, he didn't feel like an outsider dragged into someone else's war.

He felt… chosen.

The Order Fractures

Location: The Inner Sanctum — Alps, Hidden Order Citadel

The chamber was cold — not from lack of heat, but from design.

Black marble formed every surface, polished to a mirror's sheen but absorbing light in a way that made it feel like the room devoured illumination rather than reflected it. Twelve figures sat in a circle, robes trimmed in the crimson thread that marked the Inner Ring of the Arcane Order. Their hoods were raised. Only one face was visible.

Dominic Kael.

He did not wear a hood. He never had.

Where the others bowed in symbolic reverence to Vel'takar, Kael met the flame with his own fire — ambition masked as loyalty. His presence was deliberate. His voice always calm, and his strategies always three moves ahead of those around him.

A symbol pulsed behind him — the ever-watching Eye of the Order, flame-wrapped and unblinking.

The room trembled with sudden cold as the temperature dropped unnaturally. A gust less wind stirred the candles.

Then — the voice came.

Not from Kael. Not from any throat in the room.

From the walls. The marble. The marrow of their bones.

"One has failed."

Vel'takar's tone was not loud. It didn't need to be. It bled into them, corrosive and absolute.

Kael remained still. The others shifted, some visibly flinching. One even trembled.

A flicker of smoke materialized in the center of the table — no heat, just swirling ash that formed the outline of a man. A robed priest. Then flames erupted across his image and consumed it in silence.

"The guardian was not offered. The path remains sealed."

A pause.

"Trust has been... wounded."

Kael cleared his throat, subtly assuming control.

"We are aware of the failure. The small town priest acted outside directive. He was not sanctioned."

"He bore your mark."

Kael didn't flinch. "He was misguided. The old faith lingers in pockets of our Order — reverent fools confusing prophecy with autonomy. But we have not forgotten your will."

Another long silence.

"Then act."

The voice dissolved.

The temperature returned to near-normal. The shadow on the floor faded.

The others began speaking — overlapping strategies, blaming factions, arguing protocol.

Kael raised a single hand.

Silence.

"We were close," he said. "Closer than we've ever been. The Guardian is real. She breathes. She moves. And she begins to understand."

One of the hooded figures spoke. "And yet we have no eyes on her. Nora… the intern. She has gone dark."

Kael tapped a screen beside his chair. A glowing signal marked a pulsing dot — isolated, moving, erratic. "She is not lost. We embedded a tracker in her drone controller, buried beneath six layers of shielding. Not even she knows."

Another voice. "Then why not reestablish contact?"

Kael looked at the symbol burning faintly on the wall. "Because I suspect we may still need her."

A beat.

"She's not a zealot. She's a survivor. And survivors adapt. If she turns back to us willingly — she's more valuable than any soldier."

The room went still again.

"And if she doesn't?" asked the figure directly across from him.

Kael smiled faintly.

"Then we reclaim her by force. Or we use her to lead us in."

His gaze shifted toward the dying image of the priest, still flickering in faint embers.

"We've lost pawns before. But the board remains ours."

Nora's Reckoning

Location: Safehouse – Upper Room, Night

The drone controller sat on the table like an accusation.

Nora had disassembled it twice. Not because it was malfunctioning — but because something felt… off.

She leaned forward under the dim light, fingers methodically checking each circuit housing, each module — the way she always did when her mind needed order. The others were below, finishing what passed for dinner. Jack had offered her some. So had Harper. She'd declined both.

Too many thoughts.

Too many lies.

Nora pried the final shielding panel loose — and there it was.

A wafer-thin disc, buried beneath the mesh of wiring. Not a transmitter. A pulser. Subdermal frequency range — low power. Untraceable by common scans.

A tracker.

Her breath caught. The bastards.

All this time — they'd been watching. Not through her actions, but through her presence. A backup plan. Insurance. Not trust — never that. They didn't even tell her it was there.

Her hands trembled slightly as she sat back. The tracker reflected in the lens of the drone's optical relay — like a second eye, always watching.

You're not one of them. That had been Sarah's voice, weeks ago. Offhand. Casual. *You're too curious for that.*

Nora wasn't sure then.

She was now.

Everything she'd seen — from the glyphs, to the star map, to the vault beneath the temple — had chipped away at the Order's foundations. They claimed to seek truth. But they feared it. Twisted it. Controlled it.

Sarah didn't control anything. She *followed* it — sometimes recklessly, sometimes blindly, but always toward something greater than herself.

And Nora had followed too. Even when she was supposed to sabotage.

Her hand hovered over the tracker.

I could crush it now. Kill the signal.

But they'd know.

She wasn't ready — not yet. Not before she figured out what that next move would be.

Still…

She placed the tracker into a small lead-lined compartment in her field kit. Enough to block it. For now.

Then she stared at the controller, stripped and vulnerable.

So much like herself.

The weight settled on her shoulders. Heavier than armor. Heavier than orders.

She wasn't an operative anymore.

Not truly.

And whatever happened next — she would choose it.

Not the Order.

Not Kael.

Sarah.

A quiet knock came at the door. Jack's voice on the other side. "You good?"

Nora cleared her throat. "Yeah. Just… cleaning up."

She reassembled the drone controller slowly — and tucked the sealed tracker deep into her pack.

Not destroyed.

But not forgotten.

As she stood, something in her chest shifted. Not guilt.

Resolve.

Broken Trust, Chosen Path

Location: Safehouse – Main Room, Early Morning

The fire had burned low overnight — just coals now, casting orange light that painted the walls in soft shadows. The team sat in a loose semicircle, still groggy from half-slept shifts and battle fatigue. Coffee steamed in mismatched tin mugs. No one spoke much.

Nora stood at the edge of the room, just beyond the circle. Her hands were steady. Her face — unreadable. But inside, she was splitting open.

She cleared her throat.

Jack looked up first, instinct sharpening in his eyes. Sarah followed, blinking. Harper didn't move, but his gaze locked in — like he'd been waiting. Victor, arms crossed, didn't bother to hide the suspicion in his expression.

"I need to say something," Nora said.

Jack gestured toward the fire with a flick of his fingers. "Go on."

She stepped into the light. No dramatics. Just words she hadn't thought she'd ever say.

"I wasn't sent here by the university. I mean… I was. But not only by them."

Sarah leaned forward slightly, her face tightening.

"I was placed," Nora continued. "Embedded. As a passive asset for an organization you now know as the Order. I was told to monitor Sarah's work — not interfere unless necessary. Just track, report, stay close. But when you found the box, when the plateau lit up, when you solved the first lock…" Her voice cracked and she paused, steadying it. "Everything changed."

Jack's eyes were hard. "Changed how?"

Nora looked at him. "I stopped believing them. I stopped trusting what they said about the stone — about people like Sarah. About Guardians and Sanctari. About truth."

Victor's tone was dry, cutting. "That must've been convenient."

She turned to face him directly. "No. It was hell. Watching Sarah risk herself for something bigger than any of us while I stood there with a lie strapped to my spine."

Sarah's voice was soft. "You saved me. Twice. You've stood with us every step since the plateau."

Nora's lips pressed together. "Not every step. There was a tracker — hidden in the drone controller. They didn't tell me it was there. I found it last night. Disabled it."

Silence. Thick. Tangled.

"I didn't know what loyalty meant," she said. "Not until I saw what you were willing to sacrifice. What you were willing to trust."

Harper finally spoke, his voice calm but firm. "You always sounded like a cop's nightmare. Half-truths with just enough conviction to pass."

She met his eyes. "And now?"

He exhaled slowly. "Now you sound like someone who's scared she picked the wrong side. Which is the first step to picking the right one."

Victor wasn't convinced. "Words are cheap."

"I don't want forgiveness," she said. "I want a chance to earn it. To make it right."

Sarah stood then, walking slowly to her.

"You lied," she said plainly. "But I always believed there was something real about you. Even when I didn't know what it was."

Nora's eyes shimmered — but she held herself straight. "There is."

Jack nodded slowly, but his eyes never left hers. "You walk with us now. You stay where I can see you."

Nora gave a tight nod. "Understood."

Victor grunted, but didn't object.

Sarah touched her shoulder — gently.

"Then let's finish this."

And just like that, Nora was part of the circle again.

Not forgiven.

But chosen.

Before the Ascent

Location: Exterior, Just Beyond the Safehouse — Later That Morning

The team moved in silence, packs shouldered, weapons checked, eyes harder than they had been days ago.

Snow drifted in soft sheets across the low ridge as they prepared to descend from the safehouse valley. The final path awaited — carved not just in stone, but in purpose.

Sarah adjusted her scarf, casting one last look back at the weathered building behind them. They hadn't just rested here. They had changed.

Beside her, Nora tightened her grip on the newly configured drone controller — stripped, rewired, honest now. Harper offered her a curt nod. Not approval. Not yet. But something close to trust.

Victor walked ahead without looking back.

Jack waited at the edge of the trail, gaze sweeping the horizon. "Let's move," he said. "The last lock won't wait."

They followed him into the wind.

And the mountain answered in silence.

Chapter Twelve: The Sanctuary and the Stone

Beneath the Sleeping Mountain

Location: High Mountain Pass — Midday, Windswept and Remote

The mountain stood like a forgotten god, cloaked in cloud and bone-white snow, its face obscured by time and frost. No roads led here. No maps marked it. Only a single line in a half-burned journal, a vague sketch on a star map, and a vision in a Guardian's dream.

They reached the edge of the pass as the sun broke the ridge, casting long, wavering shadows that stretched like fingers across the ice.

Sarah stopped first, her breath catching.

"It's here," she whispered.

No doubt this time. No hesitation.

Jack moved beside her, scanning the blank face of the mountain. There was nothing. No path, no visible entrance, just jagged rock, and a slow wind that moaned through narrow crevices like a warning.

"This place is dead," Victor said behind them, his voice low.

Harper squinted, shielding his eyes. "Feels like it's waiting."

Nora, silent until now, stared at the slope, something shifting behind her eyes — not fear, but reverence. "The others never found it," she said quietly. "Because they weren't supposed to."

Sarah took a step forward, one boot crunching into untouched snow. "The mountain hides the last lock. I saw it in the dream. It's beneath."

"How do we get in?" Jack asked.

She didn't answer. Not with words.

Instead, she pulled the stone — *the one passed down through visions, trials, and blood* — from her pack. It pulsed faintly in the dim light, almost reluctant. Then, slowly, it warmed.

Sarah turned in place, letting the stone guide her hand. And then — just at the edge of the ridge, nestled in a crack of shadow and frost — she found it.

A single spiral glyph, nearly buried in ice, carved directly into the mountain itself.

She touched it.

The ice retreated like breath on glass.

A narrow opening formed — vertical, jagged, and just wide enough for a person to slip through sideways.

Jack's weapon was already in his hand. "If this is the last one… then whatever's guarding it won't be subtle."

"No," Sarah said, stepping through. "It won't."

Inside, the light dimmed fast. But the stone's glow didn't waver.

It pulsed.

And the mountain began to breathe.

Echoes in the Deep

Interior – The Passage Beneath the Mountain, Moments Later

The tunnel narrowed quickly, forcing the group into a single line — Sarah at the front, stone in hand, its glow steady but low. The walls were unnaturally smooth, almost polished, their curvature forming a perfect cylindrical shaft bored into the earth.

"There's no tool that could've carved this," Victor muttered. "Not in this shape. Not in this era."

Jack grunted. "Which means someone — or something — made it for a reason."

Sarah paused at a fork — one path dipped sharply down, the other sloped around in a slow arc.

Her eyes flicked to the stone. No pulse. No light shift. Only stillness.

"This way," she said, pointing toward the steeper descent. She couldn't explain why — just that it felt right. Not a pull this time. More like a memory surfacing before it was hers.

The deeper they went, the warmer the air became. Not hot, not uncomfortable — but alive. Like the mountain was exhaling from some secret place far below.

Nora, walking third in line, paused and ran her fingers along the stone. It wasn't just smooth — it was humming. She didn't say anything. Not yet. But she'd felt this before. The resonance. At the vault.

Jack noticed. "You alright?"

"I'm not the one this place is speaking to," she replied. "Just listening to the echoes."

Sarah stopped abruptly.

Before them, the tunnel opened into a massive hollow. Not a chamber. Not a vault. A *throat.* The walls widened into a vertical shaft plunging into darkness so deep the glow of the stone barely reached the far end.

Victor dropped to a knee near the edge. "There's no bottom," he said. "Or if there is, it's hiding."

"No," Harper said quietly, stepping up beside him. "There's a path."

And there was.

Along one edge of the wall, spiraling downward like the thread of a massive screw, was a narrow ledge — just wide enough for careful feet and steady hands.

Nora exhaled. "You've got to be kidding."

Sarah turned, eyes alight. "We've come too far to stop now."

She stepped out first.

No hesitation.

Not anymore.

The others followed in silence — one by one descending into the mountain's breath, the stone glowing brighter with every step… as if it knew the end was finally near.

The path wound downward, the air growing thicker with each turn. No words passed between them now. Just the crunch of boots, the brush of stone, and the steady, pulsing glow of the stone in Sarah's hand.

Then it changed.

Subtly at first.

A flicker in the light. A brief distortion — like heat rippling off pavement.

Sarah paused, fingers tightening around the stone. Her breath caught.

And then —

A vision.

Not vivid. Not overpowering. But a flicker behind her eyes. A cave. A figure cloaked in gold light. A whisper:

You were born to protect the breath between silence and fire. But even guardians must choose.

It faded.

She blinked, breath still steady. "I'm fine," she whispered — mostly to herself.

Jack saw the tension in her posture and moved forward.

But he didn't speak.

Because it hit him next.

A sharp crack of pressure behind the eyes — like altitude sickness, but deeper. Memory that wasn't memory.

A child, abandoned in a fire-lit courtyard. A blade handed down from an unseen hand.

You stand not between the danger and the door, but beside the one who must pass through it. You are the echo of resistance. The blade that remembers why it was forged.

Jack stumbled slightly — caught himself.

He said nothing. But his eyes flicked to Sarah, softer than before. His chest felt heavier — but clearer. Like some armor he didn't know he wore had begun to crack open.

Behind him, Harper stopped mid-step.

He grunted. "What the hell—"

But it wasn't pain. Not exactly.

It was a feeling he hadn't known he'd buried.

A hallway. A hospital bed. A stone left on his table.
A voice that wasn't quite a voice:
You were never meant to carry the burden. But you were always meant to arrive.

He didn't breathe for a second.

Then he muttered, "Well, screw you too," to no one in particular, and kept walking.

Victor raised an eyebrow but didn't comment.

Nora, trailing behind, felt only the silence.

And in that silence, something strange bloomed — not understanding. Not purpose.

But clarity.

They were being called.

Each differently.

But all to the same place.

The spiral continued downward.

And at the bottom, the path finally leveled — opening into a chamber carved not by hands, but by history itself.

The spiral passage leveled out into a broad corridor, smooth and wide, lined with ancient stone that shimmered faintly beneath the flickering light of the stone Sarah carried.

No torches. No glyphs. Just polished walls that narrowed into a silent mouth — and beyond that, something deeper.

They stepped into a chamber that was larger than expected — not massive, but *complete.* Its walls curved upward into a natural dome, every surface smooth and untouched by time or weather. It was too perfect to be accidental. And too silent to be welcoming.

Sarah exhaled slowly.

"This is it."

She didn't know how she knew — but she did. Every step into the room confirmed it.

The others stood quietly, taking it in.

Jack's hand flexed against the grip of his rifle — not from fear, but instinct. Not a weapon to be drawn… but something to be set down, maybe. He didn't understand the impulse. He didn't need to. He just felt it.

Harper's eyes moved along the walls, looking for seams, exits, threats. But his pulse had slowed. This wasn't a battleground. Not yet. It was… something older. A sanctuary of sorts, but not for them.

Victor stood with arms crossed, his brow furrowed in a way that wasn't entirely tactical. He looked at Sarah, then at Jack, then back toward the narrow tunnel they'd emerged from — like he'd missed something, or maybe just seen too much.

Only Nora hadn't entered fully.

She lingered at the edge, her hand still near the drone controller, gaze scanning the ceiling with quiet reverence — and guilt.

Sarah moved slowly toward the center of the room.

There, waiting, was a low altar of obsidian. No symbols. No glowing script. Just a single indentation carved into its surface — round, deep, and waiting.

Sarah swallowed hard and looked back at them.

"It's not locked," she said quietly. "It's listening."

Jack stepped forward, slowly.

Harper followed, more wary than awed. Victor stayed back a beat longer, then joined them.

And for just a moment, no one spoke.

The chamber breathed around them. Or maybe it was them — realizing that everything they'd seen, everything they were — had brought them *here.*

Not to find the Stone.

But to be ready for it.

The Final Lock

Interior – Sanctuary Chamber, Center Altar

Sarah placed her hand above the circular indentation on the altar, but didn't touch it. Not yet.

The chamber was absolutely still.

Not dead, but listening — the kind of silence that waits to be broken only by truth.

She looked at Jack.

Then Harper.

Then Victor.

Each stood without speaking. Each one changed by this place, whether they realized it or not.

The stone in Sarah's hand pulsed — a faint rhythm that matched her breath, her heartbeat… or maybe something older within her.

She touched the altar.

The reaction was immediate — not loud or bright. Just *real.*

A low hum passed through the stone beneath their feet, like the mountain itself had taken a breath. A soft glow spread outward from the point of contact, lines of light forming a series of concentric circles that spun slowly — gears of memory turning in silence.

Jack moved closer. Not to interfere, but to witness.

The pattern shifted again — aligning.

Then something remarkable happened.

Three beams of faint light emerged from the center and swept toward each of them — Sarah, Jack, Harper.

And then the altar spoke.

Not aloud. Not through sound.

But within.

A voice in each of them — different, but the same.

To Sarah:

You are the memory and the marrow. The key. The last of the line. You will not ask the Stone for power — you will offer it purpose.

To Jack:

You are the shield. The unwavering. The blade not drawn in wrath but in love. You are the Sanctari. You will bleed before you allow the Guardian to fall.

To Harper:

You are the echo of will — unchosen, yet still called. You are the sanctified wanderer. The one who chose duty even when forgotten by the world.

The beams faded.

Sarah stumbled back a step, eyes wide, hand clenched at her side.

Jack caught her — not in alarm, but instinctively.

"I'm alright," she said, voice shaking. "It… spoke."

"Spoke?" Harper echoed. "You mean like… *in your head*?"

Sarah nodded.

Victor stepped forward now, his voice low. "What did it say?"

Jack didn't answer.

Neither did Harper.

But Sarah turned to them, blinking past the light that still clung faintly to the walls.

"It said… we're ready."

The altar shifted — its top sliding back with a sound like stone being swallowed by time.

Inside: a recess, lined with cloth older than the language it was once wrapped in.

Resting at the center: a thin metallic object — not a key, not a weapon.

A blade.

Small. Curved. Forged of something that shimmered like obsidian dust caught in sunlight.

Sarah reached for it, then paused.

"I think this unlocks the Stone's chamber," she whispered. "But not by cutting anything."

Jack narrowed his eyes. "Then how?"

She met his gaze. "By cutting *ourselves*. A piece of truth. Or sacrifice. Or… something we're not ready to give."

A heavy silence hung in the air.

Harper looked down at the blade. "Well… that's not ominous at all."

Descent to the Heart

Interior – Lower Access Tunnel, Beneath the Sanctuary

The corridor was unlike the others.

Here, the carvings ceased. No glyphs. No marks. Just polished stone, worn smooth by time or purpose.

The air was different too — not stale, but *still.* Heavy. As if whatever lay ahead pressed back, even from behind sealed doors.

Their footsteps echoed in quiet rhythm.

No one spoke.

Not yet.

Victor walked point, weapon lowered but ready. Jack followed beside Sarah, his movements just slightly closer than usual — protective, but not caging. Harper took up the rear, favoring his right leg but moving without hesitation. Nora walked just behind him, quiet, her face unreadable.

At last, the corridor opened into a vast stairwell — a spiral, descending around a deep shaft cut into the mountain's core. Railing less. Exposed.

A cold draft curled upward from below, coiling around their necks like breath from something sleeping far beneath.

Sarah paused.

"I know this place," she whispered.

Jack turned to her. "From where?"

"My dream," she said. "But… it's not just memory. It's like it's been waiting for me. Like it *remembers* me."

Harper muttered, "This place doesn't just give you the creeps. It gives them *context.*"

They began their descent.

Step by step.

Each level they passed was marked by a faint change in temperature, in pressure, in *feeling*. And in Sarah's chest, the Stone pulsed stronger.

At one landing, she faltered.

Jack steadied her. "You alright?"

She nodded, but didn't speak.

It wasn't pain. It was resonance. Like tuning forks vibrating in perfect harmony.

When they reached the final level, the passage ended in a sealed doorway. Unlike the others, it was featureless — no symbols, no handle. Just a wall of slate-like material that shimmered faintly under their lights.

Sarah stepped forward and reached for the small blade she now carried in a cloth wrap.

Jack put a hand on her shoulder. "You sure?"

She looked at him — really looked at him — and in her eyes was the weight of every answer they hadn't spoken.

"I'm not sure of anything," she said. "Except that we're supposed to be here."

She unwrapped the blade, held it in both hands.

Then drew it gently across her palm.

The cut was shallow. Clean. But as the first drop of blood struck the surface of the wall, the stone *shivered.*

Lines spread outward — geometric, precise, forming an intricate seal that pulsed once.

And then, the wall receded silently, revealing the entrance to the chamber beyond.

A faint glow spilled out.

Amber. Warm. Alive.

The chamber was ahead.

The Stone… waited.

Reflection Before the Threshold

They stood in silence at the edge of the light, the open chamber ahead pulsing softly — like a heartbeat waiting to be met.

No one spoke.

But inside each of them, something stirred.

Sarah

She clutched the cloth that had held the blade, blood still fresh on her palm. The sting reminded her

she was real. Present. *Chosen.*
She thought of the dreams. The glyphs. Her father's scribbled notes. All the years spent chasing meaning through excavation and dust. And now — this.
She no longer needed to *translate* her purpose. She could *feel* it.
And yet… she wasn't only the Guardian.
She was Sarah. Still afraid. Still unsure. But ready.

Jack

He kept his hand close to the sidearm at his hip — not out of threat, but out of habit.
Every instinct in his body told him this was the edge of something final. A battle not of guns or tactics, but something older.
He thought of the mission. Of how Harper had appeared at the safehouse like he belonged — and somehow, *did.*
He thought of Sarah.
The pull toward her no longer felt like interference. It felt like destiny.
He didn't believe in fate.
But he believed in her.
And maybe that was enough.

Harper

His leg ached like hell. Always did in the cold.
But the pain was grounding. He welcomed it.
He wasn't supposed to be here. Not in this. Not with *them.*
But when the Steward had stood at his bedside and left that impossible stone behind... everything changed.
He had seen war, and lawlessness, and loss.
But never purpose. Not like this.
He didn't know if he was Sanctari. He just knew... he couldn't let Sarah walk in there without him.
He'd see this through. Even if it killed him.

Victor

He stood near the rear, fingers flexing on his rifle grip. Always watching.
He trusted no one. Not even himself, sometimes.
But damn if these misfits hadn't earned his respect.
Especially her.
Sarah Collins. The girl with dirt under her nails and the weight of ancient prophecy in her chest.
He didn't believe in stones. Or gods.
But he believed in action.
And he'd fight like hell to keep her alive.

Nora

She held the reprogrammed drone controller in her hands, thumb tracing the corner where the tracker used to be.

They hadn't asked her to come this far.

She had lied. Betrayed.

But when she saw Sarah bleeding to open that door — she hadn't seen a mark to be studied.

She'd seen hope.

For herself.

For all of them.

She wasn't Order anymore.

She wasn't even sure what she was.

But she *was* going in there.

The chamber pulsed again — brighter this time.

Sarah stepped forward.

No one stopped her.

Because they were no longer just a team.

They were a purpose.

And the Stone was waiting.

The Final Door

Interior — Sanctum Chamber, Deep Twilight

The chamber pulsed like a held breath.

Sarah stepped forward, the echo of her boots swallowed by the velvet stillness of the room. The stone walls, warm and curving, radiated a low hum — not mechanical. Alive. Like the chamber itself was aware of their presence, and waiting.

In the center stood the structure they had come so far to find.

It wasn't a door in the traditional sense. Not a slab of stone or archway. It was a **barrier of light** — a shimmering veil hanging motionless between two curved pillars, both etched in symbols only Sarah could read.

And she did.

Not consciously — not word for word — but **completely**. The script rippled across her skin like memory. Ancient glyphs wrapped around the twin pillars, burning faintly in a copper glow. She knew this was the final lock.

Jack stood just behind her. "Is that it?"

She didn't answer right away. She stepped closer. Her fingers hovered just shy of the edge of the light — not touching, but close enough to feel its warmth buzz across her bones.

"Yes," she said finally. "This is it."

Victor's voice came low and steady. "We're not alone."

Harper turned. No movement. No shadow. Just instinct — the kind drilled into men who'd spent years expecting the worst. He raised his weapon slowly, scanning the entry they'd come through.

Jack stayed focused on Sarah. "What do we do?"

Sarah glanced to each of them, then stepped back.

"I think I have to go in alone."

No one protested. Not yet.

She continued, voice calm but sure. "This whole journey… it's been leading here. And each lock, each test — they were meant for me. They *let* me through. They won't do that if you're with me."

Nora's jaw tightened, but she didn't speak. She knew Sarah was right.

Jack stepped forward. "What if you don't come back?"

Sarah smiled — soft, sad, and resolute. "Then I'll find a way to make sure you still do."

Jack hesitated. For once, words failed him.

She turned to go.

But before her hand reached the light, she stopped. Not from fear — but recognition.

Her hand was already glowing.

A faint, golden shimmer curled from her palm — the mark of the Guardian. It wasn't a burn or a tattoo. It was *truth* made visible.

Sarah stepped through the veil.

There was no sound.

No flash.

Just **silence** — and then she was gone.

Outside the light, no one moved.

Victor lowered his weapon.

Nora took a step closer to the shimmering barrier. "She made it through."

Jack exhaled slowly, but didn't take his eyes off the veil. "She was always meant to."

Harper turned away from the door. His eyes were already scanning the room, the walls, the dark corners.

"She's in," he said, "but we're not done yet."

From deep within the sanctum, a low **chime** rang — not mechanical.

Organic.

Ancient.

The lock had accepted the Guardian.

But what waited beyond… might not.

The Heart of the Stone

Interior – Beyond the Veil, Timeless Light

Sarah stepped through the shimmering veil and into silence so complete it felt like the world had stopped breathing.

She didn't fall. She didn't stumble.

The chamber on the other side wasn't a room in the conventional sense — it was a **sphere** of radiant stillness. No walls. No ceiling. Just light, stretching endlessly and softly pulsing with color that shifted the longer she stood in it — golds to blues to violets, then back again.

She looked down.

There was no floor — but she stood firm. The ground beneath her feet responded like water that refused to ripple.

At the center of the sphere hovered a structure. Not large. Not elaborate.

A stone — unlike any she had seen — **levitating** above a pedestal of translucent crystal. The stone was warm, not glowing, but emanating a rhythm. A *heartbeat.* Her heartbeat.

Sarah stepped forward.

Each motion felt *unbound.* Weightless, like thought propelled her more than muscle. The closer she came, the louder the rhythm grew — not in sound, but in *knowing.*

This was the **Eternity Stone**.

It wasn't impressive. It didn't scream power.

But it radiated a presence that bent the air itself. Like time bowed around it. Like truth was layered within it, waiting to be asked the right question.

She reached out — and it responded.

Not by flaring. Not by humming.

But by *speaking.*

In her mind. In her marrow.

You are not here to claim. You are here to choose.

Sarah froze. Her breath caught — not from fear, but recognition.

"I'm ready," she whispered.

Then you must understand. Power is not granted. It is mirrored. And what you see — will see you.

The light dimmed around the chamber.

And then, for the first time… the **Stone opened**.

Not physically. Not with a hinge or a crack. But with a bloom of vision — cascading images across Sarah's mind like a memory unspooling:

- A vast battlefield of ancient Guardians, falling beneath flame that screamed without sound.
- Stewards cloaked in white, bearing secrets across continents, chased by shadows that looked like men.
- Sanctari standing alone in flooded ruins, holding a door closed against a force that burned without heat.

And in the center of it all: **Vel'takar** — not a figure, but a **will**, lashing at the world like fire chained too long.

Then — a whisper.

Not from the Stone.

But from something behind it.

"Shall I be loosed?"

Sarah's eyes snapped open.

The Stone was still before her.

Silent.

Waiting.

"No," she said, voice trembling but firm. "Not today."

And then… it pulsed once. Bright. Final.

The chamber faded.

The veil shimmered behind her.

And Sarah turned back — carrying the Stone, and the choice, with her.

The Return

Exterior – Temple Threshold, Early Twilight

The veil split like mist in reverse.

Light parted — and Sarah stepped through.

She didn't speak. Not at first. Not as the veil closed silently behind her, its shimmer dissolving into the stone once more. The change in her was immediate — not visual, but *felt.*

Jack stood first. His rifle lowered. His voice caught in his throat.

Victor whispered, "Is that…?"

Harper moved slowly, lips tight. "She's got it."

And she did.

Cradled in both hands, wrapped in a cloth of ancient weave that hadn't existed before she crossed

— the **Eternity Stone** rested with impossible calm. No glow. No hum. Just gravity.

Sarah looked at them each in turn. Not as a leader. Not as a chosen one.

But as a *witness.*

"It's awake," she said simply.

Jack stepped forward, eyes locked on hers. "Are you alright?"

She nodded — then hesitated. "I don't know what I saw in there. Or maybe… I do. But I'm not the same."

Jack's jaw flexed. "You don't have to be."

Victor was still staring at the cloth-wrapped stone. "Is it dangerous?"

Sarah shook her head. "Only if we fail."

Harper grunted. "That's reassuring."

But even he couldn't mask the awe in his voice.

Nora came forward last, slower than the rest, expression unreadable. "What now?"

Before anyone could answer, the air shifted.

Not with wind — but with weight. With stillness.

A glow rose near the center of the chamber, not from the Stone, but beside it — soft at first, then sharp, outlining the silhouette of a figure not entirely bound to form.

The Steward had returned.

He was taller now. Clearer. No longer the indistinct presence Harper had glimpsed in the hospital. His face bore the softness of age, but not weakness — only memory. His robes shimmered faintly with light, the color of starlight on snow.

Everyone could see him.

Jack instinctively stepped in front of Sarah. Victor's hand drifted to his sidearm. Nora's eyes narrowed. Harper tensed — then relaxed, just a fraction, as if recognizing something older than trust.

"You have reached the final gate," the Steward said, voice low and resonant. "And still, you ask… what now?"

No one answered.

He turned to face each of them.

"You were never meant to open the Stone," he said, gaze falling on Victor. "Only to guard the one who could."

Then to Harper. "To bring them together — though you didn't know why."

Then to Jack.

"You feel the weight in your bones. The instinct to protect what you do not yet fully grasp. That is Sanctari blood. It remembers, even when the mind does not."

Jack said nothing, but his jaw clenched slightly. The Steward moved on.

"This is not a weapon," he said, gesturing to the Stone. "Not a key. Not a prize. It is the balance. The heartbeat. The light placed at the center of the world when the first breath stirred the dust."

He turned finally to Sarah.

"And she is its Guardian."

Silence.

The kind that didn't just hang, but *settled.* Inside the ribs. Behind the eyes.

"She was not chosen because of skill," the Steward continued. "Nor lineage. Though both align. She was chosen because she *listens*. Because she *feels* what others overlook. Because when called, she did not demand proof — only purpose."

His voice lowered.

"She is the only one who can protect it now. And so… she must be protected. Not as a relic. Not as a leader. But as the thread that holds the rest."

The light around him began to fade.

"There is more ahead," he said. "And not all of you will walk it easily. But know this — the Stone is awake. The final lock is near. And if you stand together… it may yet remain sealed."

Then he was gone.

No flash. No fanfare.

Just absence.

They all stared at the place where he'd stood — breath held, limbs still.

And then Sarah collapsed to one knee.

Her eyes were wide open, but glazed — seeing something no one else could.

Jack rushed to her side. "Sarah—?"

She didn't answer.

A warmth enveloped her. From within. Like sunlight under the skin. The world dropped away.

And in its place…

A voice.

You are not broken, Guardian. You are whole.

It wasn't words — not really. It was meaning, pressed gently into her thoughts.

You came not to claim the Stone. But to remember it. To protect it.

She stood, in the vision, before a scorched horizon — cities hollowed by flame, oceans black with ash, people bowed beneath a shadow that wore no face. Above them all: the Stone, cracked and screaming light, chained by something without form.

This is the world without you.

Sarah turned in the vision — and saw nothing behind her but a road of fire.

This is the path if you stop walking.

Then light surged through the vision — not burning, but healing. The Stone pulsed again, whole, its glow radiating outward like a second sunrise.

This is the world you guard.

She gasped as the light faded — and her vision cleared.

The team was around her. Jack held her arm, steady but uncertain. The others looked on with a mix of concern and awe.

She met Jack's gaze, breath still shallow.

"I understand now," she whispered.

And that was enough.

Sarah held the stone up — not high, not like a trophy — but with reverence.

"Now," she said, "we decide what to do with it."

No one spoke.

Behind them, the wind shifted — not cold, not cruel. Just present.

The mountain, the chamber, the veil — all had quieted. But not the world.

The war for the Stone had not ended.

It had only just begun.

Epilogue — Stillness

Location: A windswept ridge overlooking the valley below. Dusk falls.

They didn't speak at first.

The wind had shifted again — colder now, sharper at the edges, like the mountain was reminding them they weren't meant to linger. Below, the path to the next horizon stretched long and coiled, winding into the last known region where the final lock lay hidden.

The sun had dropped low behind the peaks, scattering gold across the sky. It hit the Stone, even through its containment shroud, and for a second, it pulsed — not dangerously, not warning, just *there.* Present. Awake.

Sarah sat alone on a stone outcropping, legs tucked beneath her, the Steward's last words still echoing in her mind.

She wasn't afraid anymore.

Not of the Order. Not of what might be waiting ahead.

But of failing *what she now understood.*

She didn't carry the Stone — but it was with her all the same.

Behind her, Jack approached. Quiet steps. A slower gait than usual. She didn't turn.

"I thought you'd be asleep," he said.

"I thought you didn't sleep."

A soft smile from both of them.

He stood beside her. Looked out over the same valley. "We're close."

"I know."

Jack glanced at her — something unreadable in his eyes. "Do you believe it? That… we were chosen for this?"

Sarah didn't answer right away.

Then, softly: "I didn't. Not at first. But now…" She let the sentence drift. "Now I think I've always been walking toward it."

He nodded. His hand grazed hers — just a moment — but she didn't pull away.

In the distance, a storm moved behind the mountains, all thunder but no rain. The sound of something always building, never quite arriving.

The others stirred near the tents.

Victor was sharpening a blade out of habit, eyes scanning the skyline like he expected trouble anyway. Harper stood alone by the edge of the cliff, smoking something he wouldn't name, his silhouette lined in orange firelight. Nora sat quietly by herself, tapping through an encrypted frequency — not contacting the Order, but listening to *silence*, as if hoping the silence might speak.

Something had shifted.

They were no longer a group. They were a *unit.*

Not by rank or training.

By bond.

By purpose.

Sarah stood slowly. Her fingers brushed Jack's again. This time, she let them linger.

"Tomorrow," she said, "we finish it."

Jack met her gaze. "Together."

She nodded once.

Then turned toward the tent — toward the team — toward whatever waited behind the final door.

Above them, the stars blinked to life.

And for a brief second, one burned just a little brighter than the rest — then disappeared.

Like a secret kept. Like a story not yet finished.

Far away — beyond mountains no map remembered — a whisper moved through shadowed stone.

It was not speech. Not wind.

Just… a flicker.

Something stirring beneath the world.

The Guardian has awakened.

Then the gates must not close.

Not yet.

Character & Lore Guide

Main Characters

Sarah Collins

An archaeologist by trade, but something far more by fate. Inheritor of an ancient bloodline of Guardians, Sarah is intuitive, brave, and drawn to places and truths no map records. Her journey is not just one of discovery, but of acceptance — of who she is and what she must protect.

Jack Thompson

A former investigator with a quiet code of honor. Jack is steady, watchful, and skeptical of all things mystical — until Sarah. Chosen unknowingly as a Sanctari, his role is to protect the Guardian. Even before he understands it, he begins to feel it.

Harper McBride

Grizzled, wounded, and loyal. A former sheriff's deputy haunted by past mistakes, Harper is brought into the mission by a Steward's intervention. Though not of the ancient lines, he is a shield in his own right, called not by blood, but by resilience.

Nora Katz

An academic intern with advanced tactical skill and a concealed past. Originally embedded in the team by the Arcane Order, Nora's loyalty fractures as Sarah's power reveals itself. Her defection is as much a leap of faith as it is an act of redemption.

Victor Hale

A hardened strategist and regional expert. Victor brings combat experience and an old soul's suspicion. Though slow to trust, he respects truth when he sees it — and Sarah's presence demands it.

The Steward

An ancient being who appears human but radiates something older. Tasked by the good entity to guide the Guardians and Sanctari when the time comes. He does not interfere unless absolutely necessary — but his fingerprints are everywhere.

Factions & Entities

The Guardians

Chosen by bloodline, though most never awaken to the call. Guardians are bound to the Eternity Stone — drawn by its energy, entrusted with its safekeeping. They carry no weapon but instinct. Sarah is one of the few to awaken in her time.

The Sanctari

Not born, but chosen — called by their convictions and capacity to protect. The Sanctari guard the Guardian, not the Stone. They are fewer still. Jack and Harper are two such protectors, though only beginning to realize it.

The Stewards

Keepers of memory. Recorders of truth. Chosen when the Eternity Stone was first locked away, Stewards do not age as mortals do and are forbidden to act directly. They pass knowledge through riddles, signs, and ancient lineage.

The Good Entity

The light bound counterpart to Vel'takar. It does not fight wars, but it empowers those who will. Rarely visible, it communicates only when the Guardian is ready. A quiet force of preservation and clarity.

Vel'takar (The Loosed Flame)

A corrupting force born from the Stone's misuse in ancient times. It cannot touch the Stone but influences others to do so in its name. Vel'takar doesn't seek worship — only release. Its whisper promises purpose but brings ruin.

The Arcane Order

Founded by Callan Virelli in the 18th century after receiving a shard of corrupted stone. Originally scholars and mystics, they became zealots. Today, the Order is fractured:

- Ecclesial Faction: Religious, ritualistic, steeped in doctrine and fire. Led by high-ranking zealots and monks. Believes in Vel'takar as a divine entity.

- Corporate Faction: Operates globally through influence, espionage, and infiltration. More scientific than spiritual, they seek the Stone for power and dominance — not belief.
- The First Flame (Virelli): The Order's long-dead founder, considered a prophet. His vision created the organization's twin branches — and sowed the seeds of their eventual conflict.

Temple Lore & Lock System

The Eternity Stone

An object of incomprehensible power — neither artifact nor weapon. It heals, it remembers, it judges. To those with pure intent, it grants wisdom. To the corrupt, it offers ruin. Hidden to protect the world… or the world from itself.

The Lock System

Designed by early Sanctari and Guardians. Five sequential Locks protect the Stone. Each lock:

- Resides in a distinct geographic location.
- Is hidden behind spiritual, intellectual, or emotional tests.
- Resonates only with the Guardian.

- Includes **False Locks**, decoys constructed by Sanctari to confuse the Order.

The False Locks

Decoys indistinguishable from real Locks to outsiders. Only a true Guardian or experienced Steward can recognize the emptiness at their core. The Order has found several, believing each might house the Stone.

Significant Locations

The Plateau (Lock One)

A hidden mountaintop aligned with celestial markers. Opened by Sarah's unconscious instinct. The first step in confirming her identity.

The Cave of Glyphs (Lock Two)

Beneath a sandstone cliff. Circular, pristine, bathed in natural light. Inside, cryptic wall carvings whisper fragments of Guardian lore.

The Hollow Crypt (False Lock)

An ancient tomb corrupted by time and misinformation. Believed to be the Stone's hiding place — instead, a test and a trap.

The Temple of the Shard (False Lock & Order Origin Site)

Constructed above the remnants of Lock Four. The

place where Callan Virelli first received his visions. Now guarded by a fractured priesthood. Vel'takar's influence lingers.

The Veiled Summit (Lock Five)

A forgotten mountain sealed in ice and cloud. The final Lock. True and unbroken. Holds the entrance to the Stone's sanctuary.

The Sanctuary (Final Chamber)

Not marked by grandeur, but by resonance. No guards. No riddles. Only a sense of stillness and completion. Accessible only to a true Guardian, guided by a Sanctari, and permitted by the Stone itself.

Glossary of Key Terms

The Eternity Stone

A powerful, ancient object of unknown origin. Neither artifact nor relic, the Stone holds the potential to amplify, reveal, or destroy — depending on the soul who seeks it.

Guardian

A chosen protector, born of bloodline, called to their purpose through instinct, not training. Only a Guardian can unlock the Eternity Stone.

Sanctari

Chosen not by lineage but by conviction. Protectors of the Guardian. Fiercely loyal, often unaware of their purpose until tested.

Steward

A timeless guide. Tasked with maintaining memory and safeguarding the knowledge of the Stone. Rarely seen. Speaks through riddles, signs, and inherited memory.

Vel'takar (The Loosed Flame)

A malevolent force born of the Stone's misuse. Seeks release and domination through manipulation of others. Cannot touch the Stone directly.

The Good Entity

An ancient, benevolent counterpart to Vel'takar. Communicates only with Guardians. Guides through visions, emotion, and inherited truth.

The Arcane Order

A secretive organization founded in the 18th century. Obsessed with unlocking the Eternity Stone. Now fractured between religious zealots and modern power-seekers.

The First Flame (Callan Virelli)

Founder of the Arcane Order. Received visions from Vel'takar and created the doctrine that now guides much of the Order's religious faction.

False Lock

A decoy created by the Sanctari. Appears indistinguishable from a true Lock. Designed to confuse and mislead those who seek the Stone with impure intent.

True Lock

One of five sacred barriers concealing the Eternity Stone. Each Lock must be accessed in sequence, guided by a Guardian's instinct.

The Sanctuary

The final chamber. Where the Stone rests. Accessible only when the Guardian is ready and the Sanctari has fulfilled their duty.

The Shard of the First Flame

A fragment of corrupted energy gifted to Virelli by Vel'takar. Used to communicate, corrupt, and influence. Now sealed within the vault that birthed the Order.

About the Author

Wayne Wyckoff is a retired Deputy Sheriff, Army veteran, and lifelong storyteller. Known for his sharp wit, grounded honesty, and deep understanding of duty, Wayne brings decades of real-world experience to the page. His journey from law enforcement to author has been driven by one desire: to create worlds where courage matters, where mystery stirs the blood, and where even in the darkest hour — light is never far.

Shadow of Eternity is his third book and his first major entry into the romantic mystery-thriller genre, blending ancient codes, powerful emotion, and fast-paced adventure into an unforgettable tale.

When not writing, Wayne can be found enjoying life with friends at the recreational property he helped build — Rio Del Rancho — where tales are shared, laughter is loud, and the spirit of community never fades.

This story, like those moments, was made to be remembered

www.ingramcontent.com/pod-product-compliance
Lightning Source LLC
La Vergne TN
LVHW010639110826
845149LV00014B/2890